SEP

D0446479

Full Exposure

This item is no longer property
of Pima County Public Library
Sale of this item benefited the Library

This item is no longer property
of Pima County Public Library
Sale of this item benefited the Library

Also by Sara Jane Stone

Command Performance

Full Exposure

BOOK ONE: INDEPENDENCE FALLS

SARA JANE STONE

AVONIMPULSE
An Imprint of HarperCollinsPublishers

This is a work of fiction. Names, characters, places, and incidents are products of the author's imagination or are used fictitiously and are not to be construed as real. Any resemblance to actual events, locales, organizations, or persons, living or dead, is entirely coincidental.

Excerpt from *White Collared Part One: Mercy* copyright © 2014 by Shelly Bell.

Excerpt from *Winning Miss Wakefield* copyright © 2014 by Vivienne Lorret.

Excerpt from *Intoxicated* copyright © 2014 by Monica Murphy.

Excerpt from *Once Upon a Highland Autumn* copyright © 2014 by Lecia Cotton Cornwall.

Excerpt from *The Gunslinger* copyright © 1999, 2014 by Jan Nowasky. A shorter version of this work was originally published under the title "Long Stretch of Lonesome" in the anthology *To Tame a Texan*.

FULL EXPOSURE. Copyright © 2014 by Sara Jane Stone. All rights reserved under International and Pan-American Copyright Conventions. By payment of the required fees, you have been granted the nonexclusive, nontransferable right to access and read the text of this e-book on screen. No part of this text may be reproduced, transmitted, decompiled, reverse-engineered, or stored in or introduced into any information storage and retrieval system, in any form or by any means, whether electronic or mechanical, now known or hereinafter invented, without the express written permission of HarperCollins e-books.

EPub Edition JULY 2014 ISBN: 9780062337573

Print Edition ISBN: 9780062337603

AM 10 9 8 7 6 5 4 3 2 1

To the women who are currently serving in our nation's military or have served—thank you.

Acknowledgments

First, thank you to my wonderful agent, Jill Marsal at the Marsal Lyon Literary Agency, for challenging me every step of the way, and for finding a wonderful home for this story at Avon Impulse.

To my editor, Amanda Bergeron, your insights and suggestions made this story shine, and for that you have my humble gratitude. This story marks my Impulse debut and my first opportunity to work with Avon's talented and hardworking marketing, publicity, and art departments—thank you for your efforts. And a special shout-out to Shawn Nicholls and Gretchen Swartley. You both are awesome.

Thank you to Monica Jelden for sharing your knowledge about the timber industry. Any mistakes are my own.

I could not have written this book (or any book) without the support of my family. To my children, thank you for inspiring me every day. I promise to always protect you from scary bears.

Chapter One

GEORGIA TRULANE WALKED into the kitchen wearing a purple bikini, hoping and praying for a reaction from the man she'd known practically forever. Seated at the kitchen table, Eric Moore, her brother's best friend, now her boss since she'd taken over the care of his adopted nephew until he found another live-in nanny, studied his laptop as if it held the keys to the world's greatest mysteries. Unless the answers were listed between items b and c on a spreadsheet about Oregon timber harvesting, the screen was not of earth-shattering importance. It certainly did not merit his full attention when she was wearing an itsy-bitsy string bikini.

"Nate is asleep," she said.

Look up. Please, look up.

Eric nodded, his gaze fixed to the screen. Why couldn't he look at her with that unwavering intensity? He'd snuck glances. There had been moments when she'd turned from preparing his nephew's lunch and caught him looking at her, really looking, as if he wanted to memorize the curve of her neck or the way her jeans fit. But he quickly turned away.

"Did you pick up everything he needs for his first day of school tomorrow? I don't want to send him unprepared."

His deep voice warmed her from the inside out. It was so familiar and welcoming, yet at the same time utterly sexy.

"I got all the items on the list," she said. "He is packed and ready to go."

"He needs another one of those stuffed frogs. He can't go without his favorite stuffed animal."

If she hadn't been standing in his kitchen practically naked, waiting for him to notice her, she would have found his concern for the three-year-old's first day of preschool sweet, maybe even heartwarming. But her body wasn't looking for sentiments reminiscent of sunshine and puppies, or the whisper of sweet nothings against her skin. She craved physical contact—his hands on her, exploring, each touch making her feel more alive.

And damn it, he still hadn't glanced up from his laptop.

"Nate will be home by nap time," she said. "He'll be there for only a few hours. You know that, right?"

"He'll want to take his frog," he said, his fingers moving across the keyboard. "He'll probably lose it. And he sleeps with that thing every night. He needs that frog."

She might be practically naked, but his emphasis on the word *need* thrust her headfirst into heartwarming territory. Eric worked day and night to provide Nate with the stability that had been missing from Eric's childhood thanks to his divorced parents' fickle dating habits. She admired his willingness to put a child who'd suffered a tragic loss first.

But tonight, for one night, she didn't want to think about all of his honorable qualities. She wanted to see if maybe, just maybe those stolen glances when he thought she wasn't looking meant that the man she'd laid awake thinking about while serving her country half a world away wanted her too.

"You're now the proud owner of two stuffed frogs," she said. "So if that's everything for tonight, I'm going for a swim."

Finally, *finally*, he looked up. She watched as his blue eyes widened and his jaw clenched. He was an imposing man, large and strong from years of climbing and felling trees. Not that he did the grunt work anymore. These days he wore tailored suits and spent more time in an office than with a chainsaw in hand. But even seated at his kitchen table poring over a computer, he looked like a wall of strong, solid muscle wound tight and ready for action. Having all of that energy focused on her? It sent a thrill down her body. Georgia clung to the feeling, savoring it.

His gaze dropped to her breasts, briefly, before returning to her face. He'd rolled up the sleeves of his white button-down dress shirt, revealing the corded muscles of his forearms. From across the kitchen, she could see those muscles tensing, his hands forming fists.

Yearning to touch? To pull at her bikini strings? Or was that wishful thinking on her part? Was she so crazed with desire for the six-foot-two man with the short black hair she longed to run her fingers through that she was imagining his reaction? Maybe he was horrified that his friend's little sister looked as if she belonged poolside at a Vegas hotel. Or maybe he was so shocked he didn't know what to make of the suit she'd ordered from Victoria's Secret. He generally saw her in jeans and a T-shirt while she chased after Nate, or for the years before she'd become his nanny, her US Army fatigues.

"It's late," he said, his tone neutral.

"Eric, it's eight o'clock and it is still August. The sun hasn't disappeared behind the mountains. It's the perfect night for a swim."

Eric frowned. "The pond water is cold."

He lived on two hundred acres on the outskirts of Independence Falls, a small town in the heart of Oregon's Willamette Valley, surrounded by mountains. The water was always cold. And she loved it that way. It made her feel alive.

"It will be refreshing." Georgia paused, biting her lower lip. She had a long list of reasons not to ask. That she might lose her temporary job as his nanny came a close third to the fact her brother would kill her. But her top reason? Pushing their friendship into uncharted waters might blow up in her face.

He'd always been there for her. When she'd gone out drinking for the first time in high school and downed one too many, she'd called Eric, not her brother or her parents, for a ride. Now Eric ran a multimillion-dollar timber business, the largest in the Pacific Northwest. Yet he'd taken the time to email her every few days while she'd served overseas.

Eric Moore was her friend. But she'd been sneaking I-want-you glances at him since she was a teenager. She'd dreamed about him, fantasizing about how he would look stripped out of his business suits.

Common sense told her the safe and sensible thing was to walk out the door now without another word. Let her dreams remain in her head. Pursuing Eric could lead to disaster. But she'd witnessed tragedy and chaos firsthand, rendering her brother's demand from their conversation this morning impossible. *Settle down, Georgia*, her brother had said. But she couldn't. She refused to calmly watch her life pass her by filled with longing for a man she shouldn't want. Now that she was home safe and sound from a war zone, she was done holding back.

"Maybe you should join me," she said. "I could grab the monitor for Nate's room. The signal reaches to the pond. We'd hear if he woke up."

Heat flashed in his eyes. No, she hadn't imagined it. It had been a long time, more than a year, since a man had looked at her as if he wanted to get close enough to touch her. Still, she remembered. But Eric quickly buried the spark of desire. Shaking his head, he returned his attention to his computer screen.

"Too much work." This time his tone was tight and on edge. She could hear the longing, the wanting, but knew he was holding back because he thought it was the right thing to do. Georgia shrugged. "Suit yourself."

She crossed the kitchen, heading for the sliding door that led to bluestone patio and down to the pond. Her back was to him, but she felt his gaze on her as she slipped out into the night.

The cool air danced across her skin as she walked barefoot over the stones, down to the grass, and toward the dock. She needed this—the mountain air, the feel of the grass between her toes, the cold rush of water on her skin. She'd returned home with a burning desire to experience the world around her in short, heart-stopping bursts. She craved the adrenaline, the rush that proclaimed loud and clear she was alive. If she slowed down, she might feel all those things that threatened to overwhelm her—the pain of losing her friends, the fear that her world would never be right again. And she refused to let her experience in Afghanistan engulf the rest of her life.

Georgia ran faster, taking comfort in her body's strength, inside and out, drawing solace from her ability to push forward. Slowing down was not an option no matter how much her brother wanted her to return to the quiet life she'd led before she'd joined the army. She wanted to jump from airplanes, feel the wind in her hair as she galloped across an open field on horseback, and more than anything, she wanted to make love. Now. Tonight. She refused to wait, allowing the days to disappear.

She'd played by the rules and avoided romantic entanglements while she'd served her country, which, put bluntly, meant no sex. For twenty long months. She wanted to feel a man's body against hers, pushing inside her. And not just any man. She wanted Eric.

He'd been her brother's friend since first grade. She'd grown up tagging along, and over the years, he'd become her friend too. But they'd never had a brother/sister relationship. There had always been something between them. Something hot they'd been too afraid to act on.

Not anymore. She'd survived one long deployment in Afghanistan. She refused to settle, to stand on the sidelines of her own life. She couldn't do that, not when so many of the men and women she'd served with no longer had the chance to live, to swim, to experience the world around them—and make their every fantasy come true.

Georgia glanced back at the house. With the kitchen light on, she could see Eric standing by the sink, looking out the window. She had a long list of fantasies that started and ended with Eric. She was dying to strip him out of his business suits and run her hands over the muscles built from years of working alongside his crews. She wanted to taste him, explore every inch of his body, and witness the expression in his piercing blue eyes when he lost himself in pleasure.

But did she have the guts to approach him? To go to his room, his bed? To push him to act on the desire written all over his face?

She wiggled her toes in the cold grass. She was alive. She could do anything. She had to cling to that, remind herself over and over. Otherwise it would feel as if her world had slipped away because she'd been too weak to hold on.

Her bare feet touched the dock and she broke into a run, knowing he was watching. At the end of the wooden planks, she dove into the water. The cold shocked her senses. Her lungs contracted and her limbs went numb. But she didn't fight it. The water was like an ice-cold barrier against her memories. The images of the men and women being blown to pieces, the feeling of her friend's lifeless body in her arms as she tried to drag him to safety—it all froze in the pond's cold depths.

Georgia swam deeper, pushing herself farther, knowing she required air. But part of her needed this more. Finally, her lungs screaming, she kicked her way back to the top.

When she surfaced, her bikini bottom floated beside her. She reached behind her head and pulled on the strings, freeing her breasts from the top. Tossing both pieces onto the dock, she glanced back at the house. Eric stood in the window watching her, his expression grim. Georgia gave a little wave and dove back under.

The water felt good, but knowing she planned to go after what she wanted felt even better. She swam deeper, faster. He might turn her away. Eric was steadfast and loyal. His moral compass would probably balk at going to bed with his employee, never mind the fact that her brother was his best friend and the number two at his company. Could desire override all of that?

She pushed back to the surface for another breath of air, clinging to the hope that the answer would be yes. Either way, she'd find out tonight.

ERIC TURNED AWAY from the kitchen window and closed his eyes. Georgia was naked in his pond. Raw need had a stranglehold on him, pushing him to think with something other than his brain and follow her into the water. But common sense told him it was wrong. And he always did the right thing.

He'd taken in his sister's kid when she'd died in a car wreck with her husband last year. He'd built his father's logging business into the largest operation in the country. And he'd employed his best friend's little sister as Nate's nanny when Liam asked. It was a bad idea then, and after three weeks of living under the same roof as Georgia, it was downright treacherous.

He'd had a raging hard-on for her from day one. He went to bed dreaming about running his mouth over every inch of her petite body. Judging from what he'd seen tonight, when she'd appeared in his kitchen wearing that poor excuse for a bathing suit, her breasts were the perfect size for his hands. He'd wanted to touch them since before he even knew what to do with a beautiful pair of breasts. Now he could drive her wild.

But he couldn't lay a hand on her, especially not tonight. Liam was stopping by to see her. He hadn't told Georgia because her brother wanted to surprise her. Plus, Liam didn't want his little sister thinking he was checking up on her. But he was.

Fighting in a war—she might be a woman, but he knew for a fact she'd seen action while deployed—had changed her. Georgia had always been outgoing, but never daring.

Now it was as if she required excitement. Within two days of arriving home, she had gone skydiving and received her first speeding ticket.

Georgia needed something to keep her out of trouble until she calmed down and agreed to get help dealing with the shit she'd seen and done overseas. And Eric had an opening for a nanny. She might be a little wild, but Eric trusted her not to do anything stupid while looking after Nate. So far, Liam's plan was working. Since she'd started living at his place, she hadn't embarked on a single life-threatening adventure. Instead, she'd turned all her attention to driving him crazy. She probably thought sex was her next big rush.

It stunk that she'd decided to toy with him. But then again, she had no clue he'd wanted her for as long as he could remember. He'd valued his friendship with her and her brother too much to act on those feelings. Still did.

He shifted in his chair. His mind knew he couldn't touch her, but it felt as if other parts of his body hadn't received the memo.

Eric closed his laptop—he couldn't work when he couldn't concentrate—and headed for his bedroom. Unzipping his pants, he sat on the edge of his bed, the one he slept in alone every damn night. Liam would be here soon, and he didn't plan to greet him sporting a hard-on for his sister. Christ, if Liam saw her in that skimpy suit, or splashing around in the water without it, he'd put two and two together and start throwing punches. And Eric would deserve every hit.

Reaching inside his boxers, he freed his erection. He wrapped his hand around himself and closed his eyes. He pictured Georgia in his kitchen, walking toward him, pulling at the strings to her bikini. In his mind, she sat on the edge of his large, oak kitchen table, leaning back, offering him the view of a lifetime.

The things he could do to her on that slab of wood. He imagined what it would feel like to run his hand over her pale skin from her neck, down between her breasts, his fingers moving lower and lower until they found her wet, slick, and wanting. The mental picture pushed him close to coming.

Eric groaned and picked up the pace, his hand holding tight, moving up and down his shaft. Moisture beaded at the top. He captured it, using it to lubricate his movements. It wouldn't be long now.

The soft sound of a door sliding open invaded the quiet. He felt a rush of night air, and the hand holding his dick stilled. He opened his eyes and looked toward the sliding glass door that led from his master bedroom to the patio.

Georgia stood there, a towel wrapped around her body.

What the hell? He kept his bedroom doors closed and locked. His housekeeper must have left the glass doors unlocked. He moved to cover himself.

"No, don't stop," she said, her eyes fixed on the hand trying to stuff his hard-on back into his pants.

"You shouldn't be here, Georgia," he said, his voice strained. "You need to go. And next time, knock."

He watched as she bit her lip and cocked her head to one side. Long strands of her brown hair, wet from her dip in the pond, disappeared down the front of her covering. Her fingers toyed with the top of her towel. He didn't see signs of bikini strings, which meant she'd left her suit on the dock. Knowing she was naked beneath that towel nearly pushed him over the edge.

"What if I stay?" she asked softly.

"I can't touch you," he managed through clenched teeth.

She slid the door closed behind her and turned the lock. "Then don't."

He saw something devilish flash in her brown eyes. The next thing he knew she'd let go of her towel. It pooled on the floor at her feet, leaving Georgia bare-ass naked in his room.

Eric sat on the bed, speechless, his eyes roaming over her body. He'd been right about her breasts. They were perfect. The tight peaks of her dusty pink nipples pointed right at him. His jaw clenched. He wanted to pull her close and run his tongue over her, drawing one breast into his mouth, grazing her nipple with his teeth before moving on to the second.

Georgia walked toward the foot of his king-size bed. Slowly, as if she didn't want to startle him, she crawled onto the edge. His last few working brain cells told him to get the hell out of there. But he couldn't move.

"No touching," she said. "I promise."

She shifted, swinging her legs around and spreading them wide. She planted her feet on his mattress. If he reached out, he could wrap his hand around her ankle. Hell, he could probably get both hands on her legs and pull her onto his lap.

Eric dug his hands into his comforter.

"Look at me, Eric," she demanded. "Follow my hand."

Resting back on one elbow, he watched as she ran her fingers down over her chest. Her head practically hanging off the edge of his bed, she traced a circle around her navel before moving lower still. She paused, her index finger running back and forth over the neatly trimmed strip of hair at the top of her mound.

"I want you," she said softly. "And if this is as far as you're willing to go, I'll take it."

"No touching," he repeated, his voice hoarse.

Her finger dipped between her smooth folds. "Not each other."

"It's not right, Georgia." He shouldn't see her naked, never mind watch her touch herself. It was wrong on so many levels, but the tiny shreds of willpower he'd been clinging to since she arrived in his home had fled the room the minute her towel hit the floor.

She didn't say a word. Shifting on the bed, she lay flat, her head resting on the edge. He watched as she reached her second hand between her legs and parted her lips, exposing her slick, wet entrance to him. She slipped one finger inside and moaned.

No longer thinking clearly, Eric freed his throbbing dick and started moving his hand up and down, never once taking his eyes off her fingers. Her thumb teased her clit, brushing back and forth in soft, swift circles. He memorized every moment, wishing he could replace her hand with his tongue and use the knowledge to make her come against his mouth.

She pushed a second finger inside. Slowly, she drew them in and out, allowing him to see every movement. She was wet, so damn wet.

Georgia lifted her head, but she kept her hands between her spread thighs. "You like to watch."

"Hell, yeah." When it came to Georgia, he had a feeling he'd like just about anything. But this? Watching her pleasure herself on his bed—it took him to a whole new level of turned on. It was kinky. And yes, that appealed to him too. He was consumed with the need to touch, but he couldn't. Not now. Not ever.

Tonight—Georgia in his bed with every inch of her body exposed—was a one-time thing. She'd broken his self-restraint when she'd walked into his room, catching him literally with his pants down. But that didn't mean he wasn't going to take this moment for himself. This was his only chance to see the woman he'd wanted damn near forever wild and unrestrained.

He stood, never taking his eyes off her hands, the way her back arched and her hips lifted to meet her fingers.

"Eric?"

He heard the vulnerability in her voice. The fingers brushing back and forth against her clit slowed.

"Don't stop, Georgia," he said, standing over her. "Roll over. I want you on your knees. Let me see every inch of you."

He looked up at her face. The mischievous gleam he'd seen in her eyes when she'd first entered the room returned. Without a word, she rolled to her stomach, thrusting her ass into the air and spreading her knees wide on the bed.

The view—it stole his breath away. Her fingers never stopped working, pushing in and out, her body rocking against her hand. His gaze ran up her torso, lingering on her breasts as they brushed back and forth against the comforter. Her cheek rested on the bed and her eyes were open, staring back at him.

Years of pent-up, carefully controlled desire rose to the surface. Everything he wanted for his purely selfish pleasure lay within his grasp. He stepped forward, his straining erection inches away from her entrance. Christ, if only—

"I'm going to come," he murmured. His hand moved faster, tighter. What they were doing might be wrong, but right now, in the moment? He wanted this, even if he couldn't touch her.

He came hard. On the bed, he heard a soft murmur of appreciation. He looked down and saw Georgia writhing, her eyes locked on him.

"My turn," she whispered. "Don't look away."

"I couldn't now, even if I wanted to." He wanted to witness her climax, watch her fall apart. Her hands moved faster, her body jerking and bucking wildly. She moaned, biting her lower lip.

"The things I want to do to you," he murmured. Seeing her like this, his imagination ran wild. The mental picture of Georgia on her knees, her lips wrapped around him, made him want to start back at square one minutes after he'd exploded.

"Come for me," he demanded. He might not be the one touching her, but he refused to stand by and observe. He had to be a part of this. "*Now*, Georgia."

His command pushed her over the edge. She held his gaze, her expression one of surprise, as if the orgasm had crept up on her unexpectedly.

"Oh, God," she gasped. And then she went limp, her knees splaying out farther until she lay flat on the bed, still struggling to catch her breath.

For the first time since she'd returned home, he felt as if he was seeing beneath her walls. The openness he saw there—it leveled him. He ached to pull her into his arms and hold her as she fell apart, to show her he was here for her.

"Eric?" A familiar voice called from the front hall.

Every muscle in his body tensed. "Shit, Georgia, your brother's here."

Chapter Two

THE ORGASM HIT her like a tidal wave. One minute she was watching Eric run his hand up and down his cock, his eyes glued to her. A moment later she was spiraling out of control, a total free fall into a climax that touched every part of her. She trembled from head to toe, completely at the mercy of her own pleasure. This feeling— it was her entire world. She closed her eyes as her body pulsed with life, rejoicing in it, loving it.

"Did you hear me? Your brother's here."

Georgia opened her eyes. Eric stood at the side of the bed zipping up his pants, his expression grim. Looking at him, seeing the regret in his eyes, pushed a button somewhere inside her, the one labeled "Emotions. Do not touch."

She'd shared something with him she'd never shared with another person, something intimate and private. She wasn't a virgin, though it had been far too long since she'd been with a man, but she'd never put herself on display like this. She'd never given herself an earth-shattering orgasm while someone watched. This was hands down a first.

And it had left her feeling. The physical she could handle. She needed it, craved it like the air she breathed. But the emotional? She'd been running hard from that since she returned home.

After all she'd seen overseas, all the people she'd lost, opening her heart and letting someone in wasn't an option. It would take away the small shred of security she relied on to get herself from day to day without falling apart. Right now, she could trust in herself. She was strong. She could get herself through today and the day after that. She didn't need to rely on anyone else.

Looking away, she pushed herself off the bed.

"You go ahead." She tried to keep her tone light, as if what they'd shared hadn't shaken her to her core. "If you keep him in the kitchen, I'll meet you there after a quick detour to my room."

Eric nodded and headed for the door.

"And Eric?"

He looked back over his shoulder. "Yeah?"

"Please don't tell Liam."

From across the room, she felt his body tense. It wasn't that she feared her brother knowing she'd fooled around with Eric. She might be scared of her feelings, but she could hold her ground when it came to Liam. But she worried it would hurt Eric. She'd seen the regret in his eyes. He always, always did the right thing—until tonight. Until her.

"I wasn't planning on it," he said.

The door closed behind him. Georgia picked up her towel and made a dash for the stairs leading to her second-floor bedroom. When she got there, she scrambled to find underwear, shorts, and a T-shirt. Dressed, she reached for the knob and paused.

Eric's voice drifted up. She had to go down there. Liam would be concerned if she didn't, and the last thing she needed was her brother asking questions. But facing Eric? How could she look at him and not picture the raw desire she'd witnessed in his eyes? It was a heady, powerful thing knowing she could bring him to his knees without laying a hand on him. If she'd ever doubted he wanted her the same way she wanted him, she didn't now.

But she couldn't risk a repeat performance. This wasn't like jumping out of an airplane. This wasn't an adrenaline rush she could walk away from unscathed. After she came, she'd wished she could curl up in his arms and let him hold her. Wanting that simple comfort left her flat-out vulnerable.

She refused to be weak. She hadn't come home alive and whole only to crumble. No, she had to find her way through these overwhelming emotions before she could open up to someone else, even a man who'd been her friend for years—and just revealed he could be so much more.

"Where's Georgia?" Liam's voice carried through the house's open spaces.

She quickly made her way down the curved front stairs, past the sprawling open living area to the kitchen.

Liam stood by the granite counter, his hands shoved into the pockets of his work jeans. The two men looked like night and day with Eric in his dress shirt and suit pants, and Liam in his ripped gray T-shirt and dirt-covered work boots, though physically they were roughly the same size, both large and imposing.

"I'm right here," she said. "What are you doing here, big brother? Checking up on me?"

She saw the grim expression on her brother's face, and a small tremor ran through her. Not fear, just awareness. Liam always greeted her with a smile. Always. Tonight, something was wrong.

"Nah, I came to see your boss." Liam studied her for a minute as if he could tell if she'd done something wild just by looking at her. Then her brother turned his attention back to Eric. "We have a problem."

Georgia stole a glance at Eric. He looked nothing like a man who had experienced an orgasm worthy of the Richter scale. There was no way her brother could guess they'd been naked together on Eric's bed when he arrived, not from the severe expression on Eric's face.

"A problem?" Eric crossed his arms in front of his chest with his feet firmly planted a hips' distance apart. This man could take on anything.

"Forest fire."

Georgia had grown up in timber country. Forest fires were serious business. Hearing those words, she could practically smell the smoke the memory was so strong. When she was six, her family had been forced to evacuate, leaving their home and all their worldly possessions in the fire's path. In the end, the firefighters and loggers had held the flames back before the fire reached their home. Others hadn't been so lucky. She looked to Liam, knowing he remembered too.

"Where?" Eric demanded.

"The hundred acres in White Rock."

She watched as Eric went pale. That was the piece of land he'd inherited from his father. Those trees had been growing for seventy years, maybe more. Georgia knew he'd finally decided to harvest them not because he needed the money but because it was the best time for the trees. And he also wanted to set the money aside for Nate. Eric had told her that he planned to place the profits in his nephew's trust fund.

"What happened?" Eric asked.

"Best I can figure, the lightning that passed through the area last night struck a tree," Liam said.

"It didn't rain on your side of the hill, did it?"

Liam shook his head.

"So the fire is on the other side of the property from where you were working?"

"It's everywhere now. The wind has blown it around."

"No way to know right now," Eric said. "If it wasn't started by a lightning strike, then a chainsaw must have let off a spark. You didn't see anything?"

"No. But we were moving quickly. I had a feeling the fire threat would be raised in the next day or two and we'd be left loading trucks or sitting on our hands, unable to harvest. I was pushing the crew, and somehow we missed the smoldering. It's my fault."

Georgia wrapped her arms tightly around her torso to keep herself from rushing over to her brother and hugging him tight. Liam hid it well, but inside she knew this was tearing him apart. To be responsible for a fire, a force of nature that could claim lives and ruin homes—no one deserved to shoulder that alone.

"My land, my crew, my responsibility," Eric said. "I should have been out there with you. How bad is it?"

"We're going to need to put in a fire line," Liam said. "I called the fire department and the department of forestry on my way here. They're going to come at it from one side, and I told the chief I'd talk to you about cutting the line on the other."

Georgia bit her lip. Cutting a fire line meant felling trees to stop the flames from jumping, and digging a trench. It would take all night, probably well into tomorrow. She knew the men would work fast to keep the fire from spreading. She prayed it would be enough to keep the neighboring communities safe.

But either way it would be a while before Eric came home again, longer before they had a chance to talk about what had happened earlier.

Eric headed for the hall. "I need to change into work clothes. Wait here and then we'll go."

Liam turned to her, his brown eyes filled with concern. "You sure you're OK? You don't look like yourself."

No, she wasn't OK. Not even close. "Just thinking about all those people who might be forced to leave their homes."

Liam's mouth formed a grim line. "We're going to do everything we can to keep them safe."

"I know you will," she said.

His eyes narrowed. "Are you sure there isn't something else bothering you?"

There was. The emotional fallout from one mind-blowing orgasm. But she wasn't about to share that fact with her brother. And compared with a forest fire, her problems seemed small and irrelevant.

"I'm fine," she said.

"Have you been sleeping?" Liam asked. "Are you having nightmares again?"

"I'm sleeping," she said. *Sometimes.*

Not much scared her now. Not jumping out of planes or driving too fast. But sleep? The nightmares were so vivid, so terrifying, she often woke barely able to breathe. And those were the good nights.

When she'd been living with Liam, there had been times when she hadn't woken up fast enough. The nightmares had held tight to her, and she'd screamed her heart out. He'd ripped her away from the dreams, begging her to wake up. If her screams terrified a grown man like Liam, what would a small boy like Nate do if he heard them?

Georgia didn't want to find out. Since she'd moved in with Eric, she'd done her best to sleep only when thoroughly exhausted and then only for a few hours at a time. So far, it had worked. To be safe, she'd also asked for a room on the other side of the house from Nate. In Eric's sprawling timber-frame home, it was a simple request to accommodate.

"I'm fine, Liam," she said. "Don't worry about me. You have a fire to deal with. Focus on staying safe."

"Always," Liam said.

Eric strode into the room. He'd traded his tailored office clothes for a pair of faded jeans and plaid flannel, sleeves rolled up to reveal the strong muscles of his forearms.

"I'll ride with you," he said to Liam. "While you drive, I'll call and have the chopper ready. A flyover will give us a better idea where to put the line and set up the base camp. And I'll call the crews. We'll take shifts." Then Eric turned to her. "You'll have to get Nate up, fed, and ready for school."

Georgia nodded. She could do all of those things. She didn't want him worrying about Nate while out cutting trees in the middle of the night with a forest fire bearing down on him and his men.

"But I'll be back to take him to school," Eric said.

"I can do it."

Eric shook his head. "I'll be here."

The men headed for the front door and Georgia followed. Eric paused, waiting for her brother to step out into the night, before turning back to her.

"Georgia," he said softly, "when I get back, we need to talk."

She waited until he disappeared into the darkness before shaking her head. Talking was the last thing she wanted to do. She needed things to go back to the way they were before she'd walked into his room and dropped her towel—before an emotional tidal wave had threatened the walls she'd constructed around her feelings, destroying the sense of security that kept her going from one day to the next. And she had to keeping going. She'd lived. She owed it to those who didn't make it to find her way forward, not fall apart.

BY SEVEN ON Tuesday morning, Eric was running on fumes. He'd worked through the night, felling trees alongside his crew. If they held off the fire, he'd come back and salvage the downed trunks for timber. It wasn't ideal. Nothing about a raging forest fire was.

He walked through the base camp and nodded hello to the men, who raised their hands in greeting, but he didn't stop to talk. Smoke hung heavy in the air, and there was no mistaking the smell of burning fir trees. The mood at the camp was solemn, and no one expected chitchat. In the distance, he could see the fire jumping from the crown of one tree to the next.

It was heartbreaking to watch. His grandfather had bought this land, and Eric had grown up caring for those trees. He'd worked alongside his father, limbing them to prevent something like this from happening. One damn spark and it all went up in flames.

Eric looked away, scanning the camp. Volunteers had set up a table with to-go boxes of coffee, bottled water, and food. He headed over. If he was going to take Nate to school, he needed caffeine.

"Hey, man, you headed out?" Liam asked.

He must be more exhausted than he thought. He hadn't noticed his friend's approach. Eric nodded, filling a paper cup with lukewarm coffee.

"You might want to come straight back. The wind is changing directions," Liam said. "The fire chief is talking about evacuating homes to the east."

"I heard. Talked to him an hour ago. I'll be back as soon as I can." He had to get Nate settled first.

Liam nodded. "If you have a chance, check in with Georgia. She seemed off last night. I'm afraid she is going to do something stupid."

Too late for that. She'd found her latest rush. Him. Part of him was glad Georgia had come to him. It was physically safer than jumping out of planes, and the thought of her hitting on some random guy…damn, that felt like a punch to the gut. But hell, for all he knew, she'd been seeing half the men in the valley since she'd been home.

"I'll check on her," Eric said, stirring his coffee. He felt like a teenager, but he had to ask. "Do you know if she is seeing someone?"

The muscles in Liam's jaw jumped. "She better not be. She's not ready for that. If you hear different, tell me."

Eric looked off into the distance where the orange flames danced on the tops of the trees: a physical reminder of how one mistake could destroy something that had taken decades to grow, like a friendship.

"I'll beat the crap out of any man who tries to take advantage of her right now," Liam added. "You'd do the same."

"I would." But not for the same reasons. Eric had taken advantage all right. Sure, she'd come on to him, dropping her towel in his bedroom. But he should have walked away. And shit, he should tell Liam. The guilt was one more thing weighing him down.

"Keep an eye on her for me," Liam said. "She barely listens to me. But you? She'll pay attention."

His mind flashed to the image of Georgia on her knees heeding his commands. She'd listened. And if Liam found out, he'd have his balls.

"I've got to get going," Eric said.

He headed for the makeshift parking area. Since he'd ridden over with Liam last night, he'd arranged for one of his crew to leave a company truck for him. After working through the night, driving would take all of his attention. He'd caught an hour of sleep at the base camp his men had set up and had woken up hard, dreaming about replacing Georgia's hands with his mouth. He ached to taste her. Instead, he had to go home, take Nate to school, and then tell his nanny last night had been a one-time thing.

Eric pulled into the attached garage and headed for the entrance to the kitchen. Not bothering to take off his dirt-covered boots, he opened the door and called inside. "Is Nate ready?"

His blond, blue-eyed nephew raced into the room holding a pair of stuffed frogs. "Look, Uncle Nate, two froggies!"

"Only one of those can go with you to school," Georgia said, following Nate into the kitchen. She wore the same thing as always, jeans and a plain gray T-shirt. This one read Army across the chest. Only today, knowing how she looked beneath the clothes, just the sight of her made him ache. Shit, he should be too tired after working through the night to even think about sex. And it sure as hell wouldn't help the conversation he planned to have with her later.

"New froggie," Nate said, carefully setting old froggie on one of the kitchen chairs.

"Got your bag?" Eric asked.

"Right here." Georgia thrust the child-size backpack into his hand, careful not to touch his skin.

"Thanks. I'll stop back after I drop him off, and then we'll talk."

Georgia shook her head, pressing her lips together. "Eric, you don't have to."

"Yeah, I do."

Eric led Nate to the car and buckled him into his car seat. The minute they pulled onto the road, Nate started talking, sharing every thought that popped into his head. Eric tried his best to follow along and comment when necessary. Over the past few months, Eric had learned that life with a three-year-old was one endless monologue.

Once they'd parked and unloaded, Eric took his nephew's hand and headed for the door. "Ready for your first day of school, buddy?"

Nate stopped and looked up at him, his expression too damn serious for such a little kid. "Is my mommy watching?"

Eric pinched the bridge of his nose and closed his eyes before crouching beside his nephew. In the first six months after the accident, he'd told Nate that his mother and father would always be watching. He'd thought it would help him cope, not that he knew shit about how a toddler dealt with losing both parents. "Yeah, buddy. She's watching. Your dad too."

Nate nodded, his solemn expression vanishing in an instant, replaced by a smile. "I'm ready."

Twenty minutes later, after his nephew was settled into his new classroom and happily playing trains with another kid, Eric drove out of the school parking lot and headed for home.

He couldn't stop thinking about what Liam had said. Georgia had looked "off" last night, ready to seek out a new thrill. Liam's words confirmed what Eric had been thinking—Georgia hadn't wanted him, just another rush.

His grip tightened on the steering wheel. Last night was wrong on many levels, but he sure as hell had wanted Georgia. If anyone else had pulled that stunt, he would have walked away.

He shook his head as he turned into the driveway. Georgia was an emotional mess. Liam was right on that front. And the fact that she turned him inside out with need didn't matter.

Eric pulled into the garage, turned off his truck, and headed for the kitchen. The smell greeted him at the door. Bacon. He followed it inside, stopping to remove him boots. He should probably take a shower first, but his stomach objected, especially when he saw the spread Georgia had laid out on the table—fried eggs, the yolks runny just like he liked them, buttered toast, hot coffee, and a whole pile of God's gift to hungry men everywhere, bacon.

But all the bacon in the world couldn't change the fact he had to tell the woman he was dying to get his hands on that last night couldn't happen again.

Chapter Three

"SMELLS GOOD IN here," Eric said, hovering in the kitchen doorway.

Georgia stood by the fridge, pouring a cup of juice. She appeared calm and in control, nothing "off" about her. Maybe she'd gotten it all out of her system. That thought—it should have led to relief, but it didn't.

"Sit and dig in," she said. "I know you haven't eaten anything since what? Lunch yesterday?"

"I had a donut last night." Sometime after he'd caught an hour's sleep and woken up aching for her.

He pulled a chair out from the table and sank into it. It felt good to sit after cutting down trees all night. He piled his plate high and picked up his fork. Georgia claimed the seat across from him. Quietly sipping her coffee, she watched him eat. Three bites in, he paused, knowing he had to do this now. He had to set things straight between them. "About last night—"

"We don't need to have this conversation. It won't happen again."

"It can't," he said. "I'm your boss, your friend, and Liam's friend. And Georgia, that's where we need to draw the line."

She shook her head. "You don't need to explain."

"After what we did, believe me, I do. If we start something and Liam found out..." Eric shook his head.

"Liam's my brother. Not my father or my keeper."

Eric looked her straight in the eye. He had to make her understand. He had to do this right. But he didn't want to hurt her. "He's my friend. He trusts me, believes I'll never take advantage, never touch you."

"You didn't. If anyone took advantage...I did. I shouldn't have come on to you like that," she said, shaking her head. "Especially not like that."

"It's not that I didn't like what we did." He had a feeling he'd remember the way Georgia's hands moved over her body for a long time. And every time the image popped in his head, he'd be left wanting.

She studied her coffee. "It was too wild. Just too much."

"No." His voice was firm, but in the back of his mind he knew she wasn't talking about the kink factor. He had a feeling last night had overwhelmed her. Add that to the list of reasons he couldn't go there again. Still, he refused to let Georgia blame herself. "Hell, if the circumstances were different, I'd be on my knees begging for a repeat."

She raised a single eyebrow. Back when they were growing up, he'd always envied her ability to give a look that basically called bullshit without saying a word.

"I'm serious, Georgia."

She cocked her head to one side and studied him as if she could read his mind. Maybe after all these years, she could. "I always figured you were straightlaced."

"I am. But not when it comes to you. I like you, Georgia. And I'd be lying if I said I wasn't attracted to you. But none of that changes the fact last night was a one-time thing."

She nodded. "It was. I just needed…something."

"OK then." He'd said what he had to say. Hell, he'd said more. He hadn't planned on revealing he was attracted to her. Still, they were on the same page.

But there was one question he was dying to ask. After his conversation with Liam this morning, he had to know.

Eric reached across the table and took her hand. The feel of her skin, warmed from her coffee mug, made him ache with a bone-deep need to touch her. He'd held her hand before. But after seeing all the places he couldn't go, this simple skin-to-skin contact drove him wild.

"Why me, Georgia?" he said quietly. "After all these years, knowing what's between us, why me?"

GEORGIA HAD BEEN living in a constant state of need for his touch. And now that he held her hand with his calloused fingers, made rough by long hours of physical work, she was suddenly thrust back to that exposed place. Her emotions quickly rose to the surface while her body silently begged for him to stroke her everywhere, not stopping until she came on his kitchen table.

She withdrew her hand and looked away.

"Why'd you come to my room?" he pressed.

She couldn't tell him she'd wanted him forever. If last night had made her feel emotionally weak, saying those words, admitting she had fantasized about him for years, would be like painting a bull's-eye on her heart. Biting her lip, she hesitated, searching for an explanation. "It's been a long time for me. For sex, I mean. I've had orgasms…" God, she was making a mess of this. "But not like that."

"Proximity. You needed a rush, and I was there. I get it." He sat back in his chair. "I guess it is safer than jumping out of planes."

No, not by a long shot, but she kept her mouth shut.

"But I can't be your next big rush," he added.

"I know," she said, unable to hide the frustration in her voice. "We're clear on that."

He reached for the bacon. "So what's next on your adrenaline hit list?"

Georgia blinked. Did he really think it was that easy? That she had a list of things to check off to prove she was alive and worthy of moving on with her life? That if she made it to the end she'd be fine after all she'd seen?

"It's not like that," she said.

He crossed his arms in front of his chest. "Then why are you doing this? Seeking out one big hit of excitement after another?"

"You don't know what I saw."

"Tell me," he demanded.

She shook her head. No. Getting through this, moving forward, that was on her. She hadn't told anyone—not her brother, not the few remaining girlfriends she'd kept in touch with, or the military shrink—about what it was like to watch her fellow soldiers lose their lives. She couldn't. No one else could understand.

"Georgia," he said, "tell me. Please."

Georgia pressed her lips together. She didn't have the words. Not yet. Maybe she never would.

"I can't. I'm sorry. I can't do this." She pushed back from the table, picked her keys up off the countertop, and headed for the door.

"Georgia, wait." Eric was on his feet. "Don't leave like this. Please. I don't want you to do something stupid."

She spun toward him, unable to bury the thunderstorm of emotions—anger, fear, panic—rising to the surface. "Like get naked with the next guy who happens to be in my proximity?"

"Not what I meant."

She turned the key over and over in her hand, rubbing the pad of her thumb along the jagged edge. "You don't have to worry about me. I'm not going to sleep with every available guy."

She didn't want anyone else. Just him. Always Eric, with his sharp blue eyes and powerful body.

"I'm damn glad to hear that." His hands formed fists at his sides. "But after seeing what you were willing to do…Georgia, there are other ways. I want to help you, believe me, I do."

"No." Right now, she was dealing with it by burying the emotions until she was ready. Jumping from one thrill to the next, craving the physical reminders that she was alive, might seem crazy to the people around her, but it was the only way she knew how to keep going.

Turning away from him, she opened the door to the attached garage. Behind her, she heard Eric let out a frustrated breath.

"Georgia. Please." She heard the note of frustration buried beneath his even tone. "Stay. Talk to me."

"No."

Georgia stepped down into the garage. She knew she was acting childish, but right now, she needed to be somewhere else, away from him and the wanting she felt whenever they were in the same room. Opening the door to the Jeep Eric had leant her while she was working as his nanny, she slipped inside and pulled out her phone. She didn't have many girlfriends left. The ones she had kept in touch with lived in different worlds. While they'd been getting married, she'd been living in a war zone. That didn't leave them with much common ground.

But Katie Summers had always been there for her. She didn't pretend to understand what Georgia had been through, and she knew Georgia had a crush on Eric that dated back to junior high.

"Katie?" she said when her friend answered. "It's Georgia. I have a few hours before I pick Nate up. Feel like saddling your horses?"

Her friend agreed and Georgia felt a rush of relief. She needed this—girl time—someone to talk to, not about the war, but about boys.

FORTY-FIVE MINUTES later, Georgia mounted a bay quarter horse mare named Sugar. Katie rode beside her in silence until they were away from the barn and Katie's three older brothers, who ran Summers Family Trucking from the offices connected to the horses' home. Once they were out of earshot, heading for the wide-open field, Katie turned to her. "Want to talk about it?"

"I sort of hooked up with Eric," Georgia said quickly.

"*Eric*, Eric?" Katie's green eyes widened. "Explain 'sort of.'"

Kissing and telling had never been her thing. What she'd shared with Eric had been kinky, but to her, it was also special and private. "We did things that if my brother found out, he'd start throwing punches."

"Oh, this sounds good," Katie's eyes sparkled and her red curls bounced. "I'd love to do something with a man that would have my brothers throwing punches."

"I thought you were dating that guy from Portland," Georgia said, gently nudging her mount to keep up with Katie's horse.

"I was, but my brothers liked him too much."

"And that's a bad thing?"

"Always. He started spending more time shooting pool and drinking beer when he came to visit than doing anything that would cause my brothers to lose their tempers. The best ones are always the guys who leave your brothers spoiling for a fight. Trust me," Katie said. "But we're not talking about me now. Tell me more about Eric."

"Nothing more to tell. We talked about it this morning and decided it can never happen again."

Katie drew her horse to an abrupt stop. "Why not?"

"I work for him, Liam's his friend, I'm his friend—take your pick." Georgia stared at the jagged Cascade

Mountains in the distance. Somewhere out there a fire burned, threatening everything in its path, including Eric and her brother.

"Oh, and he thinks I just wanted a bit of excitement," she added.

"I've always thought Eric looked exciting."

Georgia let out a mirthless laugh. "He is. Believe me, he is. But he's also dangerous. Emotionally."

"Afraid you'll get attached and he won't?"

"Something like that." She was scared to death she'd hand over her heart, and with it, her only sense of security. Falling for him—it would strip away her strength and her independence. "But now I have to live in the same house with him."

"Quit," Katie said with a shrug. "Find another job. The man has gobs of money. He can find another nanny in a heartbeat."

"I can't do that to Nate. I can't just disappear on the kid. But seeing Eric every day...I'm not sure I can do that either."

"And you're sure you can't 'sort of hook up' with him again?"

"It's complicated," she said. "Liam is his best friend. And Eric thinks he'll be furious if he found out. I don't want to damage their friendship."

Katie shook her head. "Brothers. They always stick their noses where they don't belong. But Liam is a big boy. You and Eric are both adults, free to make your own decisions. If you want a relationship with Eric, I say go for it."

"I don't know if I can handle it." Saying those words out loud felt as if she'd forgotten a piece of body armor, leaving a part of herself exposed.

"Oh, please. You've had a thing for Eric for as long as I've known you. Have you stopped to think that maybe you owe it to yourself after all you've been through to explore this thing between you? If he hooked up with you despite what I'm guessing is a pretty long list of reasons not to, it's obvious he's attracted to you. But it doesn't have to be deep and emotional. Just have fun. And for goodness' sake, you don't have to tell Liam unless it turns serious. Believe me, your brother doesn't need to know about every man in your life."

The words sank in. Running away from what she wanted because of a few obstacles was the coward's way out. She might be scared of what Eric made her feel, but she refused to be weak.

Chapter Four

THE FIRE RAGED for two days. Eric returned home to take Nate to preschool in the mornings and grab a quick shower, but otherwise he lived at the base camp, watching as the flames destroyed the trees he'd cared for most of his life. It was gut-wrenching to witness, especially knowing the lives of his crew, the firefighters, and surrounding community hung in the balance. Finally, thanks to the herculean efforts of the men who'd worked by his side around the clock to cut the line, it was over. The fire was out. It had claimed acres of trees, but no lives or homes were lost. And it was time to go home.

After the last of his crew left and the base camp was cleared, Eric climbed into the company truck he'd kept on-site. The midday sun glared through the windshield as he drove home. He pulled into his garage and climbed down from the truck. Every muscle in his body begged for sleep. He could probably catch an hour's shut-eye if

Nate was still napping. But first he had to make a few calls. He'd been ignoring his other projects while the fire burned.

Eric opened the door to the house and froze. The counters, the floor, every available surface was covered with flour and cooking utensils. It looked as if a misguided Goldilocks had ransacked his kitchen. And she was still here, standing in the middle of the room with her back to him. Topless. Aside from her purple and black lace bra.

Shit. He didn't need this, not when he was too tired to remember all the reasons he shouldn't reach out and remove her underwear. Eric shoved his hands in his pockets and focused his attention on the floor.

"Georgia, what happened to your shirt?" He tried for the same tone he used to address Nate when he'd left his toy trains on the stairs. Tried and failed. The words came out heavy with wanting.

She spun around, a mixing bowl in one hand and wooden spoon in the other. "You're home."

"Yeah." He pulled out a chair from the kitchen table and began unlacing his work boots, doing his best to keep his eyes on his shoes, the flour-covered floor, anywhere but on his topless nanny.

"The fire's out?" she asked.

He nodded, setting his boots to the side. "It's over."

"Was anyone hurt?"

"No."

He heard the soft sound of her bare feet on the wooden floorboards and looked up. Her jeans were covered in equal parts flour and what looked like chocolate frosting.

His gaze traveled higher. Chocolate trailed across her abdomen to under her left breast. It took all his self-control not to pull her over and lick her clean.

She stepped closer.

"Georgia," he said. It was a warning.

"Oh my God, you're bleeding." She set the bowl on the table and reached for his right arm.

Eric winced. "It's just a scratch."

His entire body hurt. So much, he'd forgotten about the cut on his right bicep. Now, thanks to her proximity and the chocolate begging to be eaten off her bare skin, his lower body ached in a way that had nothing to do with forty-eight hours of backbreaking work. No, this discomfort had everything to do with the chocolate-covered, shirtless woman standing too damn close.

"What happened?"

"I should ask you the same thing," he said, pointedly looking around the kitchen. Ingredients, in containers and out, covered the marble counters. Every bowl he owned was piled in the sink. "You still haven't told me how you lost your shirt."

She stepped back and folded her arms across her chest, pushing her breasts upward. His reasons for keeping his hands off her fled the room. One lick. There was no harm in that right? He'd already seen a lot more than her chocolate-covered stomach.

"You first," she said. "You're bleeding."

Eric sighed and closed his eyes. "I was trying to move out of the path of a falling tree and a branch grazed my arm." He'd gotten sloppy, but he refused to admit that to

Georgia. She could probably figure it out. She was born and raised around loggers. "It looks worse than it is. The cut isn't deep."

"You should put something on it."

"I'll clean it up when I shower." He eyed the path of chocolate again. "Your turn. What happened in here?"

"Nate needs to bring a snack to school tomorrow morning. One of the teachers suggested muffins. Nate wanted cupcakes. So we compromised on banana bread muffins with chocolate frosting." She looked around the room as if she hadn't realized the extent of the mess until he'd started questioning her. "I thought I'd make them while he napped and we could frost them together. You know, less mess that way. Without the toddler helping."

He raised an eyebrow. "Are you sure about that?"

"I know. More is hard to imagine. I don't have a lot of experience with baking. Not in a kitchen like this." She waved at his state-of-the-art cooking space filled with stainless steel appliances. The best money could buy. Like her, he had no clue what to do with any of it. His family had been one step above Liam and Georgia's on the middle-class ladder, but they'd never had money to spend on fancy kitchen gadgets.

"Did you know you have two mixers?" she continued.

"No, I didn't. Marie handles the cooking," he said, referring to the cook/housekeeper who'd worked for him since he built the house five years earlier. He managed breakfast, or relied on Georgia, but Marie prepared everything else.

"Today is Thursday, Marie's day off," Georgia said. "So turning to her for help wasn't an option."

"Why didn't you grab something at the store?"

She picked the mixing bowl up from the table and turned back to the mess on the counter. "I thought it was important that Nate bring something homemade. The other kids, they all have moms to make their snacks."

Her words tore into him, cutting deeper than the scratch on his arm. Georgia might be struggling to deal with her issues in her own stubborn way, but she was trying her best for his nephew.

"Thank you." It was all he could manage. The emotions—gratitude, desire, grief—added to his exhaustion and overloaded his senses.

She nodded. "I'll clean up the mess. I promise. After I get these in the oven."

"Marie can tackle cleanup in the morning," he said. "Just put on a shirt. The crew will be here soon. We're having a cookout this afternoon for my guys and some of the firefighters. It starts in two hours."

Eric headed for the door, not waiting for her response. He needed to get out of here. A kind, caring, and half-naked woman spelled trouble. One more minute in this kitchen and he might forget that he couldn't touch her.

GEORGIA WEAVED THROUGH the crowd of men, careful to avoid Eric. Her palms grew clammy, and warning bells went off in her head. There were too many people between the house and the pond. Her damaged mind equated crowds with danger, an increased threat of attack.

In Afghanistan.

But she wasn't there. Not anymore. She knew that. Still, shaking the fear—it wasn't easy.

Her breaths became short and shallow. She wanted to escape, but Nate was running around, playing with one of the guys' golden retriever. The men had all tossed back a few beers, and with the pond so close, she wanted to be the one watching Nate. She headed for the edge of the green lawn down near the pond. From here, she could see Nate and run to him if he approached the water. And she could breathe again.

Out of the corner of her eye, she saw Eric break away from a group of men. She abruptly turned and stepped off the cleared, green lawn and into the wood area at its edge. She could still track Nate's movements and hear the crowd. But she wouldn't have to make small talk with Eric and his buddies. Not when she was still wishing she'd kept her shirt on and her mouth shut in his kitchen.

She'd been so focused on making the perfect muffin from scratch that she'd hadn't given a second thought to stripping off her T-shirt when she spilled batter down her front. Then he'd walked in, catching her off guard. To make a bad situation worse, she'd spoken without thinking. Her words had pushed on his grief. He'd come home tired and injured. The last thing he'd needed from her was a reminder of his sister's death and all Nate had lost. But that was exactly what she'd given him.

Eric stopped by the tree line, chatting with a few of the firefighters. He had changed into clean jeans, a Moore Timber T-shirt, and cowboy boots for the picnic.

In one hand, he held a beer. To most people, he probably looked relaxed, having conquered a forest fire hours earlier. But even from a distance Georgia could see the tension in his body, in the way he gripped his beer and scanned the crowd every few minutes while listening to his friends.

Leaning against the thick trunk of a pine tree, Georgia looked away, focusing on Nate. She didn't have a clue how long she'd been standing there when she heard footsteps crunching the pine needles and fallen leaves. Her muscles tensed until she spotted Eric. He'd slipped into the trees and was moving toward her, his steps intent and determined.

"Are you all right?" Despite his broad shoulders, all six feet plus of him managed to stand in the tree's shadow, virtually hidden from the people on the grass.

She nodded. "Fine."

Eric stepped closer, transforming the open-aired space into something intimate. Their shoulders were practically touching as they both watched Nate play with the dog. Being this close to Eric, she could feel the tension she'd sensed while watching him. He was like a caged lion waiting to pounce. But just like the other night when she'd burst into his bedroom and dropped her towel, he held back.

"You sure about that?" he asked.

She shoved her hands into the pocket of her jeans to keep from reaching out and touching his jean-clad leg or company T-shirt hugging tight to his muscular arms. His presence sent her common sense rushing into battle with the need burning through her body to touch him, feel him, kiss him. She wanted to peel away his clothes to reveal the rough and rugged man beneath. She wanted—

"You're avoiding the party," he added.

"I wanted to keep an eye on Nate without the crowd distracting me," she said.

He turned and she felt him looking her over, head to toe. "I think you're the distraction," he murmured, his deep voice pushing hard against her resolve to keep her hands to herself. "I thought I told you to put a shirt on."

Georgia glanced down at the loose tank top draped over her purple bikini. The neckline rested low across her breasts, revealing part of her bathing suit. The sides were open. A strong breeze could literally blow her shirt away. But that was the style. Cutouts were in. At least according to the magazine she'd picked up in the grocery store. After more than a year of wearing the same uniform day after day, she'd wanted clothes that made her feel young and feminine.

She shrugged. "It's a cookout."

"It is." He shifted his gaze away from her shirt, looking to the clearing between his stone patio and the pond. "But if you wanted to hide, you could have chosen a better camouflage."

"I'm not hiding. Just taking a break. Too many bodies in one place makes me nervous."

Eric frowned and stepped back. One minute, he'd appeared ready to press her up against the tree. But now? Desire had given way to concern.

"I didn't realize crowds were a problem," he said.

Georgia shrugged. Sometimes she didn't know herself until she walked into a situation what would happen. After living in a constant state of high alert, it was hard to shake the feeling that a threat was always there, waiting for the right moment to strike.

She stared at Nate and the retriever. "Crowds are unpredictable. That's one of the first things they tell you when you step off the plane over there. They drill it into you. And now? Too many people in one place…it feels like an easy target."

"You're not a target, Georgia," he said quietly. "Not anymore. You're safe here."

"I know." Why was it so hard to escape the lingering fears now that she was home? She wanted to package these feelings up and ship them back to the war zone she'd left behind. It was time to move on. And it was up to her to make that happen.

Georgia turned, pressing her back against the tree. She could still see Nate playing and laughing with his new four-legged best friend, but her focus turned to Eric. Shifting against the tree, she allowed the rough bark to catch her shirt, drawing it up in the back. The front of her tank drifted down, revealing more of her breasts.

Eric followed the shirt's movements, his blue eyes narrowing. He looked as if he were one step away from reaching for her with a wild growl. But he stepped back. Georgia caught his hand before he moved outside the tree's shadow, lacing her fingers through his, holding tight.

"Are you here, checking up on me, as my boss or my friend?" she asked.

He squeezed her hand. "Your friend, Georgia. Nothing changes that, OK?"

Georgia nodded. "Good."

The promise that she would not upset their friendship cut away at the barriers. Maybe, just maybe...Her hand, still entwined with his, gave a gentle tug. But Eric didn't budge. It was as if his feet were locked in place by his strong moral code.

I'm your boss, your friend, and Liam's friend. And Georgia, that's where we need to draw the line.

His words from the other day echoed in her mind. But knowing he would always be her friend, part of her wanted to step across.

"Eric?" A man's voice cut through the trees.

He released her.

"Hey, there you are." Paul Smith, one of the local firefighters and a friend of hers from high school, approached. He walked through the trees, his sandals crunching the fallen leaves. Like the other guys who'd worked alongside Eric the past few days, Paul had taken the time to shower and change—in his case, into cargo shorts and a T-shirt—before driving over.

Eric nodded. "Checking in with Georgia. You need something?"

Paul raised his right hand and rubbed the back of his neck. Georgia's gaze went straight to his right bicep, her eyes widening. When he flexed his arm—holy cow. Paul, the kid who'd been a shrimp in high school, now had the muscles of four men. She'd met some ripped men in the army, but Paul put them to shame. But while she could admire his physique, looking didn't make her want to touch. Not like with Eric.

"Actually, I was going to ask you where I could find Georgia." Paul turned to her. "Hey. Welcome home."

"Thanks." She wrapped her arms around her waist, her fingers brushing the bare skin in the cutouts.

Georgia focused on Paul, doing her best to pretend Eric didn't command her attention just by standing nearby, towering over them. "How's your family? Is your mom still raising llamas?"

"She is," Paul said, his face transformed by a boyish grin. "My sister moved home and is helping her."

"Georgia," Eric said tightly. "You might want to check on Nate. I need you to make sure he stays away from the pond."

She looked past Paul, scanning the open grass for her charge. Since she'd taken refuge in the trees, Nate had moved closer to the house, and away from the pond.

"Before you take off," Paul said, stepped forward, reaching for her. But a quick glance at Eric and Paul dropped his hand without touching her. "I heard you're into outdoor sports. I'm off tomorrow night and was planning to hike the Columbia River Gorge, see the waterfalls, maybe camp out. I'd like the company if you're interested."

"I—"

"She can't." Eric moved to her side, placing his palm on the small of her back. It felt as if every nerve in her body rushed to greet his hand and beg him to stay, to keep a hold on her. "She has plans. I need her tomorrow. To work."

Georgia reached for anger. He didn't have a right to claim her, to steal her away from an adventure and demand that she work overtime on a Friday night. But his hand on her, and her body's needy response, said otherwise.

She struggled to find her righteous indignation. But it wasn't there. She walked into his space the other night. She'd invaded, demanding that he pay attention to the desire burning between them. He was fighting hard against it. But in this moment, he'd let it rise to the top.

"Sorry," Georgia said to Paul. "Maybe some other time."

Eric's fingers pressed into her back, a silent *hell, no*.

Paul backpedaled, moving out of the trees, his eyes darting back and forth between her and Eric. "Sure thing. I'm going to grab another beer. Take care, Georgia."

Paul disappeared into the crowd, and Eric's hand fell away. Georgia grabbed it, holding tight to keep him from vanishing into the open space.

"I have plans?" she asked. "Is that true or were you just trying to save me from an adventure?"

Eric frowned. "A long walk uphill through the woods doesn't sound exciting."

Georgia looked over at where Paul stood, fresh beer in hand, talking to his buddies with his broad back to them. "He's a firefighter. He works search and rescue in these mountains. I bet he could have carried me up the gorge."

"You'd never let him." His tone was clear and decisive.

Georgia opened her mouth to object and then closed it.

"You're right," she said finally. "I wouldn't. Not when I'm perfectly capable of reaching the top on my own two feet. And I think a climb sounds like fun."

"Georgia—"

"Maybe I should find a sitter for tomorrow and take him up on his offer." She released him and stepped toward the cleared, fresh-cut grass.

Eric grabbed her arm and she froze. "Find a sitter and I'll take you out. Hiking, climbing, whatever you want."

Georgia looked down at his fingers wrapped around her bicep and then up at his face. His blue eyes burned intense and unwavering, making her feel as if she were the only person for one hundred miles. She saw darkness and desire—as if she were seeing another part of the career-focused, do-the-right-thing man she'd known forever.

The corner of her mouth lifted, and her pulse sped up a notch. "Why?"

"Just being a good friend."

She raised an eyebrow. "Are you sure about that? I think you crossed the line."

"Not yet, Georgia." He let go of her arm, turning toward the group of men gathered around the beer. "Not yet."

Chapter Five

ERIC TURNED INTO his driveway. As the house came into view, he could no longer ignore the fact that he'd agreed to an adventure with a woman who was living and working for him. A woman he was supposed to keep out of trouble. He could tell himself he was playing the part of the concerned friend until he was blue in the face. It wouldn't change the fact that when someone else offered to take Georgia hiking, he wanted to scream: *she's mine*.

But Georgia didn't belong to anyone. And judging by the way she'd reacted to the crowd, she needed a friend more than anything. Georgia had a mountain of issues to work through. She was like a wildfire, burning out of control. He wanted to help rein her in, but he didn't want to get burned in the process.

Eric tightened his grip on the steering wheel. Whatever he felt for her, he had to bury it. Deep. As he had for the past decade.

He pressed the button on the remote. Waiting for the garage door, he glanced to his right. In the grassy area beside the house, Georgia stood in a pair of form-fitting blue jeans, cowgirl boots, and a flowing white tank held together in the back with a panel of lace. Between the boots and the frilly top, she was a picture-perfect farm girl. Holding a gas can.

Eric's foot hit the break. With the nose of his car in his parking space, he watched her fill up one of his four-wheelers. When she finished, she turned to the second. On the back of that one, he saw a picnic basket, two bows, and a quiver of arrows bungee corded to the rack.

Eric drove into the garage, stepped out of his car, and went to find Georgia. "Four wheeling to dinner?" he asked.

She turned the cap on the second gas tank before glancing up at him. "I thought a picnic would be more discreet. And this will ensure we're home before dark."

He raised a brow. "Turning into a pumpkin when the sun sets?"

"I don't want to ruin your reputation, Mr. Straightlaced."

She headed into the garage and Eric followed, watching as she rose to her tiptoes and reached for a high shelf. Her shirt rode up, revealing a slim section of her back. Mr. Straightlaced? He wasn't so sure.

His mind traveled back to the other night when she exploded in a rush on his bed. He wanted to touch her, but he didn't want to stop there. The things he wanted to do to her…

Eric shook his head, pushing the images away. It was one thing to take his best friend's little sister on an adventure, just the two of them, because he couldn't stand the thought of another man hiking and camping with her. It was another thing entirely to want dirty, downright kinky sex. And Georgia took his fantasies to a dangerous new place.

She slid the gas can onto the shelf and turned around. "Our sitter also needs to get home on the early side tonight. Katie's inside with Nate if you want to say hello and change," she said, glancing at his business suit.

He nodded. "I'll be back soon."

Inside, he found Nate and his sitter playing trains on the kitchen floor. Three bowls sat beside the track—carrot sticks, dip, and fish-shaped nuggets.

"We're having a train picnic," Nate exclaimed, springing from the floor and hurling his small body at Eric.

"Hey, buddy." Eric lifted him up and hugged him tight. Coming home to this kid—he was everything. From the day Nate moved in, every other piece of Eric's life took a backseat to his nephew—his company, his personal life, everything.

Hold that thought.

"We add a cargo car every time we finish a vegetable." Katie rose from the floor, smiling at Eric.

"Thanks for hanging out with him tonight," Eric said. "We'll be back before dark, so I can put him to bed if he wants to stay up."

"Yes!" Nate hugged him tighter.

"Sure thing," Katie said. "But don't rush home on my account. I want Georgia to enjoy her night off."

One look at the knowing sparkle in Katie's eyes, and it dawned on him. She thought this was a date. And shit, he'd gone to school with her brothers. So had Liam, not that he spent much time with the Summers brothers now, but if Katie talked...

"We're just heading out for a little target practice," he said.

Katie's smile widened. "I don't need to know the details. And don't worry, Eric. I won't tell anyone about the two of you. I promised Georgia."

"There's nothing to tell," he said, his voice firm. He set Nate down by the train picnic and headed for the hall.

Twenty minutes later, Eric pulled up alongside Georgia and cut the engine on his four-wheeler. The spot she'd picked for their early evening picnic offered a view of the valley and the surrounding mountains. He frowned. He knew this area. And this spot was not on his land. A couple from California had cleared the homesite a few years back, but then the market dipped, especially in rural Oregon. It had been empty ever since.

"You know, I own plenty of acres with good picnic spots," Eric said. "We don't need to trespass."

"No one will know, and this place has great views." She released the bungee cords securing their meal to the back of her vehicle.

"Any more surprises I should be aware of? We're not going to skydive after dinner?"

Georgia smiled sweetly. "Nope. Now we eat and shoot some arrows."

"You're the only woman I've ever met who brings a bow to dinner." He released the cords holding the equipment she'd placed on the back of his four-wheeler.

She shrugged, attaching the quiver to her belt. "I figured we could both use the practice. When was the last time you shot a bow?"

"Before Nate moved in. These days most of my spare time is spent with him, and he's too young to handle one of these. Maybe when he is older I'll teach him." He shook his head. "I'll add it to the list, which grows longer every day. There is so much I want to show him."

"You're a good dad." Georgia set the basket and blanket down. "I knew that from the moment I started living with you two."

Eric froze, the bow in his hand. "You did?"

He'd felt as if he'd been standing on the edge of parenting failure since Nate arrived. He loved and provided for him, but he wasn't sure it was enough, especially for a kid whose world had been turned upside down and inside out.

But what else was he supposed to do? He didn't have a clue. His parents were not the best role models. As a kid, he had often felt like a footnote in their lives instead of the focus.

"How?" Eric asked. "How did you know?"

Georgia turned her head to one side, studying him. And in that moment, he felt vulnerable and exposed, as if he'd showed up at a work site buck naked.

"You made Nate the center of your world," she said. "He comes first."

Eric nodded. "He does."

Georgia walked a few steps from her chosen picnic site. He watched as she set her sights on a towered pine, withdrew an arrow from the quiver, and raised her bow. "Having a three-year-old hasn't left much time for you, has it? And your personal life?"

She let the arrow fly, hitting the tree in the center.

"Is that your subtle way of asking if I'm seeing someone?" he said.

"No." Georgia pulled out a second arrow and handed it to him. "I'd know if you were. Unless you're sneaking off to a motel while we're all asleep."

Eric laughed, taking the arrow and loading his bow. "I'm not. If I was, someone in this town would find out and they'd talk."

"I didn't think so," Georgia said. "But just because you're not dating doesn't mean you can't have fun."

He turned his gaze back to Georgia. His body tightened, jumping to conclusions at the thought of fun and Georgia.

"How about a friendly competition?" she suggested. "Best out of three? Winner claims the prize."

She was talking about arrows and adventure while his lust-filled mind barreled straight across the line into a place he couldn't go, not with her.

Eric raised his bow, aiming for the arrow she'd placed in the tree. "You're on. What's the prize?"

Out of the corner of his eyes, he saw Georgia grin. "You prepare breakfast for one week."

Eric released the arrow, watching as it missed the tree. "You want to win a week of cold cereal? That's the extent of my cooking."

"Hmm, you're right." Then her smile widened, lighting up her brown eyes. "How about you have to buy me all the gumballs I want for one week?"

"Gumballs?" Eric laughed, shaking his head. Growing up, if Georgia won a bet—with him, Liam, or anyone else—she'd demand payment in gumballs from the machine outside the Independence Falls grocery. "Seriously?"

She nodded, fighting to look serious. "Old habits die hard."

"And if I win, what is my prize? A candy bar?"

"Sure." She glanced at his first failed attempt to hit the tree. "But I wouldn't start thinking about whether you want nuts and caramel or peanut butter cups just yet."

His competitive drive, which had thrust him to the top of his industry, took hold. Pushing aside everything else, Eric focused on hitting the target. But by the time the sun edged behind the mountain peaks, Georgia had three arrows embedded in the tree. And Eric had one.

He shook his head as he headed out to collect the arrows while Georgia did a victory dance. "No need to gloat," he called over his shoulder.

"Come on, every win deserves a victory dance. You and Liam taught me that when you finally let me play flag football with you in high school. And I just won a week's worth of gumballs."

He marched back to the picnic area with the arrows. "We're not kids anymore, Georgia."

Eric regretted the words the moment they crossed his lips. Every time he looked at her, he grew more and more aware of that simple fact. Her jeans hugged the curves he wanted to run his hands over. The fabric of her shirt brushed the smooth skin of her stomach and low back. Georgia was a lot of things—but she wasn't a kid.

She froze midtwirl. "No, we're not."

Her words were heavy. It was as if he'd reminded her of everything she'd seen and done, experiences that, at twenty-six, pushed her far away from childhood innocence. He couldn't begin to imagine what she'd witnessed, but he knew it had stripped away pieces of her, while at the same time adding to the woman he'd known. She'd come home wild, scared, and—against all odds—determined to push past it all. He wanted to help her find her way, but he didn't have a clue the right way to go about it.

Eric picked up the blanket and spread it on the grass. "What happened the other day at the cookout, when you hid in the trees—is it just crowds that frighten you?"

Georgia knelt and began pulling items from her bag. Fried chicken, potato salad, green beans, and biscuits. Still not saying a word, she withdrew two cans of beer and handed him one.

"Thanks." He took it, sitting on the blanket across from her. "If there is something that scares you, I'd like to know. If I'd known that crowds made you feel like a target, I would have cancelled the picnic or moved it to another location. I want you to feel safe. Always. And I want to help you through this. Let me in, Georgia. Let me help you."

GEORGIA SIGHED, SHAKING her head. The space between them felt thick, weighed down by his words. This wasn't supposed to be a night of serious conversation. But Eric knew her. Better than most. If something touched a nerve, he noticed. And unlike most people, he didn't look the other way.

She studied him, compiling her thoughts as if they were pieces to a puzzle. He leaned back on his elbow with his long legs stretched out before him. He'd changed out of his office slacks and into jeans when he got home and saw her gassing up the four-wheelers for their date. But he'd kept the crisp white button-down sleeves rolled up.

Part businessman, part rough lumberjack—it was a potent combination. She wanted to laugh and joke with him. Maybe kiss him. Not talk about what scared her or what kept her up at night, why she needed so much more out of every single day just to feel alive.

But she needed him to understand that she was handling the feelings that threatened to strip away the ground beneath her feet. She was pushing forward the only way she knew how. She didn't need to hand over her problems to him and wait for him to unlock the secret to putting the pain of losing friends, of bearing witness to death, behind her. What she wanted from him was very different.

"I'm not broken," she said, opening the prepackaged food containers she'd picked up at the store. "Yes, crowds make me nervous sometimes. But I deal with it. I just need some time to put things in perspective."

He picked up a chicken leg. "I never said you were broken."

"Broken, cracked, mentally unstable." She shrugged. "It's all the same thing. And I know Liam thinks I'm on the brink of some sort of epic meltdown. But I'm not." She would never let that happen. Whatever it took, she'd fight it.

"Can I ask you something?" Eric said.

"Sure." She reached for the potato salad, craving the familiar taste of comfort and home.

"Why'd you enlist?" he said. "After college, why didn't you move back here? I know Liam was pushing you to come home. So what made you wake up one day and join the army?"

Georgia stared at the creamy mix of potatoes, celery, and spice. Her brother had asked that question again and again. She'd always told him the same thing: because she'd wanted to, plain and simple. But there was more to it.

"I know the reason you gave to Liam," he added. "But there has to be something else. You joined knowing we were at war. You had to know it would cost you."

"I did." She looked at him. "But I didn't lose anything I can't reclaim."

Her sleep, her sense of security—she could and she would find those things again. She'd lived through it and come out whole, at least on the outside. On the inside? She could fix that. As long as she didn't push too far too fast and respected her boundaries, she could put herself back together.

"But you didn't need to go." His voice held a hint of sadness and a touch of desperation, something she rarely heard in his words. "Georgia, I'm proud of you. Knowing you were over there, risking your life, it scared the shit out of me. And your brother too. He hid it well, but Liam was terrified."

Georgia set the food aside, her appetite slipping away. "I know. And I'm sorry for that. When I graduated, I had no idea what I wanted to do. You and Liam, you both knew your future was here, waiting for you. But I didn't know where to go or what to do with my life. I needed a purpose. And I needed to do something on my own and see what was out there. The army gave me that. From the day I started basic training to the day I came home, being a solider, it challenged me."

She looked over at him, searching the strong, hard lines of his familiar face to see if Eric understood. She had a feeling her brother never would. How could she expect them to understand what it was like to be a woman who wanted so much out of life, but didn't know where to turn? She'd grown up on the fringe of the middle class and lost her parents, one after the other, to cancer while she was in college. Then she'd graduated knowing only two things about what she wanted for her future—adventure and purpose.

"And I don't want being at war to be the last big thing I do with my life," she said softly.

"It won't be," he said, his voice firm, as if issuing a command.

"Making the declaration and putting it into words are two different things," she said ruefully.

Eric stared at her, his gaze unwavering. For years, she'd craved his attention, hoping he'd look longingly at her. Not that his expression held a hint of desire right now. He was assessing, analyzing. "Do you remember when you were eight and your class adopted a child in Africa?"

Georgia's brow furrowed. "Yes. She was from a small village, and her parents were struggling to feed her and her family. She wanted to go to school."

"After school that day, Liam and I rode home with you in the carpool with Marshall Thompson. You declared that you were going to become president of the world and once you were elected, you'd make sure every girl in Africa could go to school and grow up to be a doctor. Marshall laughed at you and told it was impossible." Eric sat up, reaching for a napkin. "You tried to take a swing at him in the backseat of his mom's station wagon."

"Yeah, but we're not kids anymore, remember?" she said. "It's not that easy. And Marshall Thompson was right. You can't run for president of the world."

Eric smiled as he wiped his hands clean and set the napkin aside. He sat across from her, so close she could reach out and touch his arms, his shoulders, his chest…

"Maybe you'd be the first," he said, his blue eyes locked with hers. "I have a feeling you can do anything you put your mind to, Georgia."

His smile and the laughter in his eyes faded, eclipsed by burning intensity.

"Anything?" she said softly, her gaze dropping to his lips.

He nodded, his jaw tightening. She watched as tension rippled through his muscles. He leaned forward a fraction of an inch before catching himself, his hands forming fists, pressing into the picnic blanket.

Georgia looked up. Heat, wanting, it was all there in his expression. Her heartbeat went a notch higher. But this time, the parts of her body begging to respond to that look weren't the same ones that felt the rush when she shot arrows.

"If I can do anything…"

Her voice trailed off as she felt him intently studying her mouth. But then he shifted away, as if adding physical space would help. And heaven help her, she wanted to close that gap.

Georgia inhaled sharply. Her courage ran deep. She knew that. She just hoped it wouldn't fail her, because right here, right now, she wanted to kiss him. One kiss. It wasn't too much. She knew she shouldn't, but that didn't quiet the need, burning bright, ignited by years of wishing she could touch her mouth to his.

Leaning in, she captured his lips, kissing him lightly. Not enough to taste him. But that simple connection— her mouth pressed to his—sent shock waves through her body. Nothing else touched. She kept her hands firmly planted on the picnic blanket, and his remained at his side. She felt his lips part as if he wanted to take control of the kiss. But he held back.

His jaw tightened, his lips closing tight as he pulled away. Georgia didn't move. The firm line of his mouth, the way the muscles in his forearms tensed against his rolled-up shirtsleeves—Eric was the picture of self-restraint. But his eyes told a different story. In their deep blue depths, she saw how close he was to setting his unwavering moral compass aside and taking what he wanted.

Her.

A thrill ran through her body. Damn it, she yearned for it to, not wanting to think beyond this moment and the rush of physical desire.

"You still haven't touched me," she said, letting her words push against his resolve.

"I'm not going to." His voice sounded strained, as if holding back took everything he had.

"Eric." She tilted forward, every wild, reckless fiber of her being pushing her to demand another kiss.

His hand touched her face, cupping her cheek, gently holding her lips away from his. She pressed against his palm and closed her eyes. Slowly, she felt him draw near. But his mouth didn't find hers.

"Eric. Please. I want this." She kept her eyes shut. They were so close, his breath brushed her ear, teasing, taunting, and stirring her desire. She lifted one hand, wanting to rest it on the front of his shirt, but his free hand wrapped around her wrist, holding her away.

"You think I don't?" His voice was low and raw. "I want to run my hands over you, Georgia. I'm dying to feel the weight of your breasts. Hold them up to my mouth. I want to lick every damn inch of you. When you come

I want you to know it's because I'm touching you, tasting you."

He drew back and she opened her eyes. There was fire in his expression—threatening, exciting, and downright primal. In sharp contrast, the rise and fall of his chest remained measured and controlled. But just barely. He was holding on to control by a thread. And if she had scissors, she'd have shredded his resolve along with his shirt.

Eric relaxed his hold on her wrist, but he didn't let go. It was almost as if he knew she was thinking about undoing the buttons and stripping off the fabric. The man who'd spelled out what he wanted didn't belong in button-down business clothes.

"I want to touch you, Georgia, but I can't." He released her, pushing away and rising to his feet. "It's not right."

"Are you sure?" she challenged. "Because it feels more than right."

Eric turned away, scooped up the bows, and headed for the four-wheelers. "We should head home."

Georgia nodded. But she didn't move. Right or wrong, she didn't want to go back, only forward.

Chapter Six

Knock. Knock.

Eric went from dead asleep to awake in an instant, a skill that came with having a toddler in the house. Swinging his legs over the edge of the bed, he heard the door creak.

Georgia. Her name, the memory of her lips touching his, her question—*Are you sure?*—was front and center in his mind. He'd gone to bed thinking about her, his body still reeling from that simple kiss. He wanted her, had for years, and he couldn't flip a switch and turn it off, even if that was the right thing to do.

"Uncle Eric?"

Nate's soft voice cut through the darkness, pushing aside all thoughts of the little boy's nanny. Eric tossed off the covers, walked over where his nephew stood by the door, and crouched in front of Nate. "What's up, buddy?"

"My room is dark." His nephew wrapped his arms tight around Eric's neck. "And there's a bear."

"The bear is back?" Eric stood, lifting Nate with him, and headed for the hall. This wasn't the first time Nate's nighttime fears, which often masqueraded as bears, had woken him. But in the past, his nephew had stayed in his room, crying. The sound carried through the monitor, and Eric went in to comfort his nephew. Always. But tonight, Nate had sought him out.

"He is in your room?" Eric asked.

He felt Nate nod.

"OK, buddy. Let's check it out." Eric carried Nate up the stairs to the study he'd converted into a child's bedroom. In the corner, the frog nightlight cast a pale green glow over the blue walls decorated with train stickers.

"Where'd you see this bear?"

"Over there." Nate pointed to the bookcase. "And there." His finger moved to the child-size table. He spoke with absolute certainty. Eric nodded, knowing words would not be enough to convince his nephew the room was bear-free. He had to prove it. He gently laid Nate down in his toddler bed and pretended to search.

"The bear's gone, buddy." Eric knelt beside Nate's bed, checking to make sure his nephew still had his stuffed frog.

"Stay with me?" A little hand reached out from beneath the blankets and grabbed his larger one. "The bears might come back. But not if you're here."

The words hit Eric square in the chest. This little boy needed him. Tonight, tomorrow, and for the rest of his life. Eric didn't have the luxury of living in the moment with Georgia. Kissing her, touching her, was more than a question of right or wrong. Hearing those words, he was sure of one thing: he couldn't risk inconsistency in Nate's life.

"I'll stay."

Holding his nephew's hand, Eric stretched out on the floor beside the small bed and closed his eyes.

"Thank you, Uncle Eric," Nate murmured. Judging from his voice, his nephew was on the edge of sleep. "I'm not scared anymore."

Eric gave Nate's hand a light squeeze. "Anytime, buddy. I'll keep watch for the bears tonight. I promise."

And he'd do the same tomorrow.

Lying in the dark, his thoughts drifted back to Georgia. He pictured her standing with her bow drawn, poised to hit her target. She was an irresistible blend of power and beauty, so damn determined.

Are you sure?

Those words, the challenge in her voice, continued to haunt him. Because as much as he knew he should, he couldn't let her go.

ERIC WOKE TO sunlight pouring in the windows. His back ached from lying on the hardwood floor for most of the night, and he'd lost feeling in his left hand due to the fact that he'd held it up, clasped to his nephew's, for hours. Sitting up, he looked down at the still-sleeping Nate in his small bed. The kid looked so damn content, as if everything was all right in his world because Eric had stayed to protect him from the bears that roamed the house after dark. Eric smiled. Maybe Georgia was right. Maybe he was on his way to being a good father figure for the kid.

"Hey, buddy." Eric withdrew his hand from Nate's and reached up to brush the hair out of the little boy's face. "Time to rise and shine. I think I smell breakfast downstairs."

Nate blinked. "What day is it?"

"Saturday." Eric pushed up off the floor. "And you know what that means, don't you?"

"Pancakes!" Nate bounced out of bed, going from sleep to bursting with excitement in an instant.

"Yup," Eric said. "I'm going to get dressed, and I'll meet you in the kitchen."

Nate was out the door in a flash. Eric followed, pausing at the top of the stairs. He waited until he heard Georgia greet Nate in the kitchen before he took the steps two at a time to his room. By the time he entered the kitchen, the pancakes and bacon were on the table. Georgia stood by the coffeemaker, pouring two cups. She wore her usual jeans and T-shirt, her feet bare as she moved swiftly and efficiently around his kitchen.

"Good morning," he said.

Georgia turned and smiled at him, holding a full mug. "Just in time. Here's your coffee."

"Thanks." He took the cup, careful not to brush her fingers, and sat across from Nate. He felt as if last night had turned his world on its axis, forcing him to map out, in graphic detail, what he wanted—and then walk away.

He'd chosen the correct path, but hell, seeing Georgia, it didn't feel right.

She stood over his nephew's chair holding the maple syrup. "You're on syrup restriction," Georgia said firmly as she poured a modest serving on top of Nate's pancakes. "Your breakfast should not be swimming in a pool of sugar."

"And you"—she turned to Eric—"are on bacon restriction."

Eric set his coffee down on the table and glanced at the modest serving of bacon, then up at Nate. "She's bossy today."

The little boy didn't look up from his plate. "Because she's a solider. Soldiers are bossy."

"She told you that?" Eric reached for the syrup, following Georgia's movements out of the corner of his eye.

Nate nodded. "When I grow up, I want to be bossy too. But not a solider."

Georgia set her mug and plate down beside Nate. "He's going to be the boss of the trains," she said. "Right, Nate?"

"Uh-huh. Uncle Eric," Nate said, pushing his empty plate away, "am I still going to Grandma's house tonight?"

"If you want to," Eric said. His mother had asked for monthly sleepovers with her grandson, but he never pushed Nate to go. Eric knew firsthand how fickle his mother's attentions could be, and he didn't want that hurt to touch Nate. But he couldn't flat out refuse to let Nate see her when she lived only an hour away. The kid didn't have much family left. "I can drive you over there today."

"I want to go," Nate said. "I want to see if Grandma's dog had puppies yet."

Eric pulled out his phone and texted his mom to confirm the visit. Without Nate around, he could catch up on work or sleep, maybe both. His phone vibrated and Eric looked down at the screen. "You're all set, buddy. Grandma is expecting you this afternoon."

"I need to pack." Nate jumped up from the table, disappearing into the front room to pick out which toy trains would make the trip to Grandma's house.

"It's nice of your mom and Henry to take him," Georgia said, referencing his mother's latest boyfriend. Although Henry had been in the picture for the past few years, Eric barely knew the guy. He kept waiting for his mother to move on. She always did.

"I guess I have the night off," she added, collecting Nate's plate from the table.

"You're never required to work weekends. Not unless something comes up." When that happened, he always paid overtime. He assumed Georgia joined them for weekend breakfast because she enjoyed their company, not obligation. But the lines between work and play, boss and friend, were blurring—had been since the day she moved in.

Georgia laughed, closing the dishwasher. "Eric, something always comes up. Or at least it has since I've been living here."

"I've been busy." He'd spent the past five years buried in work, knowing every hour logged brought him closer to success. "But if you ever need a night off, tell me."

"I'll keep that in mind. You know, in case someone invites me on a hiking trip."

His grip tightened on his fork. *Hell, no.*

"I have a better idea." He wasn't about to let her walk into the arms of a firefighter. He shouldn't care one way or the other, but ever since she'd slipped into his bedroom, he couldn't escape the feeling in his gut that she was his. If he was being honest, it had started years before she dropped her towel and climbed onto his bed.

"My mom's place is halfway to the coast," he continued. "We could get out of town. Grab a bowl of chowder at the Clam Shack. Maybe stay at my condo on the beach."

She raised her eyebrows, crossing her arms in front of her chest. "Dinner at my favorite restaurant on the planet and a sleepover?"

He nodded.

Georgia ran her tongue over her lips as her arms lifted her breasts higher. Her eyes sparkled as if she were mentally mapping out her plans for their night away.

"There are two bedrooms," he said.

"I'm in. But I don't think we'll need both beds. Unless…" She shrugged. "You never know what might happen."

"Georgia—"

"I'll go find Nate and help him pack."

Her face lit with excitement and daring as she danced out of the kitchen to find Nate. Eric closed his eyes, grinding his teeth. He had a bad feeling that one night with Georgia would never be enough.

"TRUTH OR DARE." Georgia sprinkled crackers into her piping-hot bowl of chowder. Sitting across from her in a pale blue leather booth that looked like something from 1960—it probably was, given how long the Clam Shack had been around—Eric laughed.

"What are we, sixteen?" he said. "I haven't played that game in years."

"Me neither. But if I recall correctly, you and my brother once drove out here on a dare. Without permission."

He nodded. "I was grounded for weeks. Same with Liam."

"Pretty wild for a pair of choirboys," she teased.

"We were never choirboys, Georgia. We all have our secrets." He set his spoon down and reached for a pack of crackers. "Even your brother."

"Liam can keep his," she said firmly. "Right now, I think it's time for us to get a little reckless, have some fun."

The Eric she'd grown up with followed a strong moral code, always keeping him on the straight and narrow. But he'd still had fun. Over the years, he'd changed. She suspected running a multimillion-dollar business had something to do with it. So did losing his sister and becoming a guardian/father to a little boy overnight. Commitment and obligation framed his life. But tonight, she wanted him to break free from the stiff walls he'd built around his day-to-day existence.

Georgia swallowed a spoonful of chowder, savoring the rich and creamy taste. She'd come here countless times growing up, with her family and with Eric and

Liam. This food tasted like her best memories of home. The ones that had kept her going while deployed, and now that she was back, offered a sense of safety. She'd been happy here, and nothing had tainted that since she'd returned. On the coast, she could be strong, courageous, and maybe a little wild.

"Truth or dare," she repeated.

He shook his head. "You're relentless."

"I've learned to never give up." She dropped a few more crackers into her bowl.

He took a long drink from his beer. "Truth."

She held her spoon to her lips, searching for a question. Her emotions might be off the table. But his were fair game. "What are you afraid of?"

Eric looked out the window at the waves crashing against the shore. "A lot of things, Georgia."

"When it comes to us," she clarified.

"That's a long list," he said slowly.

"Start at the top."

"Hurting Nate."

Her brow furrowed. "Why?"

"I sat by his side at the hospital. After the accident. I wanted to be there when he woke up. I told him what had happened. About his parents. He didn't understand. How could he?" Eric shook his head and closed his eyes for a moment, as if the memory was too much. She knew that feeling and wanted to offer comfort, but knew it wouldn't help.

"I told him it was just us now," he continued. "I promised we'd be a family."

"I'm not trying to change that. To take away what you have with Nate. And I'd never walk away from him."

Finally, Eric looked at her. "I know, Georgia. But after my parents divorced, I hated riding their relationship roller coaster. They passed my sister and me back and forth. We were always in the way of their latest relationship. And every time we met one of my dad's girlfriends and started to like her, she left or my dad ditched her. My mom wasn't much better. She traded boyfriends the way most women switch shoes. Nate has already lost his parents. As long as he is with me, I don't want him wondering if everyone in his life might vanish."

"You're worried I'm too unstable to maintain a place in Nate's life," she said quietly.

"Georgia, I'm sorry—"

"Don't be. I get it," she said softly. "You forget that I saw the way your parents paraded their not so significant others in and out of your life. I know you, Eric. We're friends. That will never change. But other things might. If you're willing to make the leap," she said. "And then, after a while, we might be just friends again."

"You make it sound so damn simple," he said, shaking his head.

"Maybe that's what I need. Simple." She sipped another spoonful of soup. "Now it's your turn."

"My turn?"

"To ask the question," she said, hoping to move the evening back into the strictly fun column. "Truth or dare."

He laughed, the sound filling their near-empty corner of the restaurant, and Georgia felt some of the tension wash away.

"I feel like a teenager, playing this game."

"Becoming a businessman and father doesn't mean you aren't entitled to a little fun."

"OK, I'll play." Eric drained his beer and set his glass on the table. "Truth or dare."

Georgia swallowed the last of her chowder, pretending to consider the question when in truth she already knew her answer. Questions might leave her vulnerable. Tonight was about fun. Responsibility and loss had chipped away the simple pleasures in their lives like a sculptor wielding a chisel. She needed a reminder that life wasn't about the missing pieces. It could still be lived, enjoyed, and sometimes even cherished—especially here in this place that wasn't burdened with her fears and nightmares.

"Dare."

"We're in a restaurant," he said, pouring the last of the crackers into his bowl.

Georgia nodded. "Be creative."

Chapter Seven

ERIC HEARD THOSE words and knew he should walk away. But desire mixed with that one word. *Dare*. His imagination ran in ten different directions. The things he wanted to do to her, the places he wanted to see his hands move over her body, and hers over his, raced through his mind. It was like watching a highlight reel of his sexual fantasies.

But this wasn't about him.

Eric leaned across the table, keeping his voice low even though he'd demanded a table in a quiet corner of the restaurant, just in case having others around them set off warning bells in her head. "I dare you to tell me your fantasies."

Georgia's eyes widened. "A dare is supposed to be an action."

He sat back in his seat and crossed his arms in front of his chest. "Feel free to demonstrate."

She raised an eyebrow, and he wondered if she planned to take him up on his offer. If her fantasies were anything like his, a little show-and-tell would draw unwanted attention. And it might get them arrested.

She cocked her head as if debating which path to choose. Part of him screamed *demonstrate*. He could afford the bail.

"Are you done with your chowder?" she asked.

He nodded.

"Get the check," she said. "I'll tell you while we walk along the beach. Your condo isn't far from here, right?"

"Five minutes on foot." Eric withdrew his wallet and dropped a pile of bills on the table, more than enough to cover the meal and tip. "Let's go."

Watching her slide from the booth and head for the exit, knowing where this was headed when they reached the shore, the last shreds of his self-restraint snapped. It was as if he was waiting for her towel to drop again, unwilling to look away.

Eric followed her out the door and down the old wooden steps to the beach. Silently, they walked side by side. He couldn't touch her. Not yet. This wasn't a sweet stroll by the shore, hand in hand. One touch would set him on fire. He had a feeling it would do the same for her.

The sun was inching lower and lower in the sky, but it was still too bright. And even when it fell below the horizon, the lights from the condo buildings and hotels lining the shore would cast a soft glow over the beach, bright enough to illuminate two people stripping down in the sand.

Twenty paces from the Clam Shack, alone on the shore except for a man tossing a tennis ball for his dog, Eric leaned over, careful not to touch his lips to her ear. "Start talking, Georgia."

"My fantasies?"

He nodded. "Tell me. I dare you."

She shoved her hands in the front pockets of her jeans, and her eyes focused on the sand in front of her, as if she were doing her best not to step on shells or debris. In the dimming light, he couldn't read her expression.

"You're my fantasy," she said.

Eric stopped short, her words hitting him in the gut. He'd been waiting for her to describe something kinky and wild. "Georgia—"

"I don't mean wedding bells." She paused beside him and looked up, meeting his gaze.

"When I lie in the dark at night, I dream about watching you strip out of one of your suits," she continued, her voice barely audible over the rush of the waves.

Eric stepped closer, unwilling to miss a single word. But he kept his hands fisted at his sides.

"I picture you moving toward me as you undo each button, the way your muscles shift when you pull your undershirt over your head. Once you're naked, I imagine your hands reaching for me, slowly peeling off my clothes," she said, her voice low and husky. With each word, the sun dipped lower, further cocooning them in darkness. "Pulling away the layers quickly. No hesitation. And then, you'd touch me."

"Where?" he demanded. "Show me."

There was just enough light to see her fingers trace a slow path from her collarbone, over the edge of her shirt to between her breasts.

"Here." Her hand moved to her right breast, his eyes tracking her movements. Through the thin fabric of her shirt, she palmed the flesh he was dying to touch, lifting it as if she were imagining him testing the weight and fullness.

"Would I stop there?" His words were a near whisper.

"No."

He glanced up at her face, barely visible now in the dim light. "Tell me, Georgia."

"In my fantasies, you're very talented with your mouth. I've spent years wondering what if would feel like to have your tongue trailing down over my stomach, to have you on your knees, moving lower and lower."

The crash of a wave punctuated her sentence. Eric closed his eyes, tempted to rush into the water and escape the mental picture of Georgia's legs spread wide and his mouth teasing the soft folds that he'd watched her explore with her own hands.

"Is that detailed enough for you?" she asked.

"Yes." He heard the rough edge in his voice. He raised his hands, reaching for her. But she danced away. Hell, maybe she'd realized how wrong this was and planned to hightail it to the water first.

"My turn," she said.

It took him a second before he realized she was talking about the game. Through his burning need to touch her, he wondered if she required the pretense. If she did, was that a sign she wasn't ready to move beyond kisses in a field and dirty talk on the beach?

"Truth or dare," she said.

"Dare." Right now, thrust up against the limits of his desire, he craved action. And her touch. It was wrong, damn it, but he couldn't spend another night watching her run her hands over her body. It was his turn.

"Good choice." She placed her hands on her hips. "Which condo is yours?"

He pointed down the beach to a townhouse divided into two units. "The deck on the left. The one with the hot tub."

"Perfect." Excitement lit up her voice. "I dare you to take off your clothes and climb in."

He raised an eyebrow. "You'll join me?"

"Yes."

The image of her naked body pressed against his in the warm water left no room for doubts. He undid the button on his polo and pulled the shirt over his head, tossing it at her. "You're on."

He turned and strode toward the stairs leading up to his vacation home. Eric reached the wooden gate and punched in the security code to unlock the latch. He heard soft footsteps behind him on the stairs. Georgia. *His* Georgia.

Eric held open the gate, waiting for her to slip past him. A second later, the floodlights switched on, illuminating the deck. Securing the gate behind her, he moved to the hot tub, releasing the latches that held the top in place. One push and the cover slid to the ground. He withdrew a condom from his wallet, the one he'd slipped in there before leaving the house just in case tonight led them to this moment, and set it on the tub's edge.

He turned to Georgia, who was staring at his bare chest as if she wanted to devour him but could not decide where to start. That look, hell, it threatened to shut down his common sense. He needed her. *Now.*

Her fingers toyed with the hem of her shirt, distracting him. Eric reached for her, his hands covering hers, pulling her shirt off.

Purple lace. Her nipples pressed against the peekaboo fabric. His hands ached to touch. Georgia reached behind her back and released her bra. The straps slid down her shoulders, and the lace fell away from her breasts.

Eric let out a low growl, grabbing hold of her hips as he reached for her jeans. Fingers fumbled, moving quickly, releasing buttons, drawing down zippers, and racing to strip away the last pieces of clothing before they tumbled into uncharted territory.

Drawing back, Eric scanned her face, searching for any signs of doubt. Finding none, he placed his hand on her hip. Slowly, he lowered his mouth to hers. He brushed her lips, mimicking the soft kiss she'd given him in the field. But he couldn't hold back. He deepened the embrace, pouring years of wanting into this kiss.

"Georgia." He leaned his forehead against hers, closing his eyes. Running his hand through her hair, he stopped short of pressing his lower body against hers. Before they climbed into the tub, he needed her to know this was more than a game. "I've wanted you for so damn long."

Tension radiated off her in waves. She grabbed his hips and shifted hers forward, drawing her naked body against his erection. The contact blew him away. But in the corner of his mind, the one small place not overrun with pleasure, he translated her actions. She needed this to be about sex, not emotions. For her, it was simple. If she felt anything more, she was pushing it away.

Tonight, he'd take what he could get. He'd let her hide behind her games.

"Get in, Georgia," he said. "I dare you."

Chapter Eight

GEORGIA ACCEPTED HIS challenge. She moved to the wooden step leading up to the hot tub and set her hands on the edge. Glancing over her shoulder, she looked at Eric. She'd seen him in board shorts before. But still, the sight of his muscular chest, covered with a light dusting of hair, left her body humming with anticipation. And when she looked lower, to the place his shorts usually covered, she had a moment of oh-my-he's-mine-tonight awe.

Turning away, she eased one leg in, followed by the second. Warmth engulfed her lower body. Moving farther into the tub, she sank deeper until the water lapped at her breasts. Just as she'd clung to the chilling sensations in his pond, she narrowed her world until only the tingling from the hot tub remained.

Behind her, Eric climbed the steps. Georgia closed her eyes and listened to the sound of the wood creaking beneath his weight. Every detail here mattered. Nothing beyond that.

She hoped he understood. She'd meant what she'd said at the Clam Shack. She wanted uncomplicated fun, a chance to explore the physical desire that had pulled at them both for so long—on her terms.

But when he'd kissed her…

It was like a promise. But she could not push that button inside labeled Emotions. She wasn't ready.

Georgia opened her eyes and saw Eric standing on the top step, staring down at her. Leaning back into the water, she lifted her feet off the hot tub floor. She spread her legs wide as her breasts floated on the surface. She studied his expression, watching as his features darkened, suggesting a raw, physical need. Judging from the way his hands formed tight fists at his side, Eric was struggling to hold back.

"That night, in your bedroom," she said, "you said you wanted to do things to me. Show me. Now."

Eric closed his eyes. "Georgia—"

"This is just between us, Eric. Don't let the outside world in. Not here."

Her words worked like a magic spell, drawing him into the tub. He pushed away from the bench that ran around the hot tub's perimeter and sank, submerging in the water up to his chest.

Georgia drifted back, floating toward the tub's wall. Eric followed, his powerful body forcing the water aside. It was like a dance. When she moved, he followed.

"Sit up on the edge," he ordered.

Georgia placed her hands on the lip and pushed down until her bottom rose out of the tub. Her legs dangled in the water. Waves splashed against the sides as Eric pressed forward. He stopped in front of the bench. Wrapping his right hand around her ankle, he lifted it up, placing her foot on the edge.

"Don't let go," he warned, lifting her other leg.

Perched on the rim of the hot tub, with her hands firmly planted on the small space beside the corner headrest and her legs extended in a V shape with only a small bend in her knees, Georgia was completely exposed under the outdoor floodlights. Eric knelt in front of her, his broad shoulders between her limbs and his mouth inches from her core. She watched, waiting for him to reach out and touch her.

"The things you want to do better involve your hands and mouth," she murmured.

He glanced up, his lips forming a hint of a smile. His blue eyes burned bright. That look—it was unfamiliar, and entirely wicked. This was a new side of the always-do-the-right-thing man she'd known practically forever. Excitement, laced with adrenaline, rushed over her.

"Trust me, Georgia." She felt his hot breath touch the sensitive flesh that ached for him. "Please."

With her body? One hundred percent. And right here, right now, that was all he was asking for.

Eric placed his hands on her inner thighs and lowered his mouth. His tongue swept down over her entrance, exploring, tasting, before running up to her clit. Georgia closed her eyes. She couldn't watch. It was too much. But God, the sensation...

He used his tongue the same way she'd touched herself on her bed. The fact that he remembered pushed past the building physical sensations, touching someplace deep inside. But Georgia forced him out, determined to keep that part of herself on the outside of the tub. His thumb pressed at her entrance, drawing small circles, teasing her.

"Oh God, Eric," she cried out.

"You're so close," he said, drawing his mouth away from her. She opened her eyes and looked down at him. Meeting her questioning gaze, he pushed his thumb inside. "Come for me."

He lowered his mouth, brushing her clit again and again with his tongue. Georgia arched her back and cried out. She was right on the edge, so close...

Let go. Let go. Let go!

His possession, his thumb filling her, moving within her, while his mouth licked and sucked—it felt so complete. It was as if he was asking for more than she was willing to give. Through the fog of pleasure descending on her body, she knew she needed to hold some part of herself back. If she didn't, she would shatter, breaking into pieces.

"Now, Georgia," he demanded.

He flicked his tongue over her, and she couldn't hold on any longer. Giving in, she clung to the waves of physical sensations, savoring her release, and refusing to let it become anything more than it was.

Finally, as if sensing the end of her climax, he drew back.

"Turn over," he said. "Place your knees on the bench and your hands flat on the edge."

His hands moved to her still-quivering limbs as he guided her into position. She felt the water lap against the back of her thighs. Eric's fingers wrapped around her hips, holding her in place. His long, hard length pressed up against her. Georgia focused on the dark ocean.

Burning a path over her skin, Eric ran his palm over her backside to between her legs, shifting his hips back. She missed the connection until he slipped one finger inside her, testing her wetness.

"You're so ready," he murmured.

After what he'd done with his mouth, how could she be anything but ready for him? He withdrew his hand. She heard the rip of the condom wrapper, and a second later she felt his cock positioned at her entrance. In one swift move, he claimed her. Completely. Georgia closed her eyes and let go. Her doubts and worries would still be there afterward. But right now, she wanted to abandon her body to the physical pleasure. Every stroke, every touch, was rough, demanding, and close to perfection.

Behind her, Eric's movements slowed to a halt.

"Don't stop," she pleaded.

"We should move inside."

"No."

"We're visible from the shore."

She shook her head. "No."

There was a fine line between mind-blowing orgasms and overwhelming emotions. If they moved inside, away from the impulsive game that had led them to this place, she might cross the line, leaving her vulnerable.

"Wait here," he ordered. "Don't move."

She heard the splash of water and felt cold air replace the warm caress of his skin. She focused on what she could hear and see—the sound of his footsteps on the deck, the ocean in the distance.

The light vanished and Georgia blinked in the darkness. Lights from the surrounding condos seeped in over the large wooden divider between Eric's unit and the neighboring homes, casting a soft glow. Her senses adjusted, focusing on the soft splash and the feel of the water shifting around her thighs as Eric reentered the tub. The darkness brought with it a sense of safety. And she held tight to that feeling.

Eric moved behind her, placing his hands on her back, running them down to her hips. He shifted, adjusting, and then he pushed inside.

"This time," she said, "don't stop."

He started thrusting against her. "Wasn't planning on it."

The way he held her, there was no escape. Her body didn't want one, she realized as her back arched, encouraging him. One of his hands released her, dipping into the water until he touched the one place guaranteed to make her cry out and beg for mercy.

"Yes, Eric!" she screamed, not caring if anyone heard her cries. No one else mattered right now. Just Eric.

Her orgasm descended on her, swift and fierce. The sensations were perfect. And entirely too much. Even out here in the open air, under the night sky, she felt overwhelmed. Her body trembled, threatening to give way beneath her.

"I've got you," Eric said, his voice low and gruff as his arm snaked around her waist, his hips still thrusting against her as he sought his own release. She knew when he found it, felt him still behind her and heard him moan.

Georgia lowered her forehead to the edge of the hot tub, fighting back tears as the rush of feeling hit her. He could have been anyone, standing behind her, pushing her closer and closer until she shattered. But he wasn't. It was Eric, the man who'd had a hold on her heart for years.

Slowly, he pulled back, withdrawing his arm from around her waist. She sank farther into the water, keeping her eyes closed and her head pressed against the tub's edge.

Being out here, removed from the rest of the world, no longer felt safe. What they'd shared wasn't about the game or the rush. It was about her and Eric. How they had sex and where didn't change the fact that every touch pushed against her emotions. Desire, need, friendship, and something that felt an awful lot like love swirled around and around inside her like a riptide threatening to pull her under.

"Georgia?" Eric's hands wrapped around her waist, drawing her onto his lap. She went willingly, resting her head against his shoulder.

There were so many things she wanted to say. *Don't let me go. I need you. I feel so much for you, and it scares me.*

"That was the best game of truth or dare ever," she said, hoping the words would lift her back to emotional safety.

Eric chuckled. "Yeah. It was wild."

"And that works for you?" She lifted her head off his shoulder, wanting to see his expression.

"You work for me, Georgia." He tightened his hold on her, but his attention shifted to the darkness beyond the deck. "The chance that someone could have seen us, did that turn you on?"

No. She wanted to say the word, but if she did, he'd ask why she refused to move inside. And she wasn't ready to tell him about how deep her feelings ran for him and how much that frightened her.

She shrugged. "I don't mind a little added excitement. But I'm glad you turned off the light."

He didn't say anything. His hands moved over her skin, stroking her hip, running over the top of her leg, as if even now he couldn't stop touching her.

"I'm getting a little warm," she said, taking his hand in hers as she stood in the water. "Maybe we should get out?"

Eric nodded, following her out of the tub and onto the deck. "I need to call my mother. Check in on Nate." He released her, moving to a wooden storage bin and withdrawing two towels.

"I should also run back to the Clam Shack and pick up the car," he said, wrapping the towel around his waist. "You want to settle in while I'm gone? It's early and we have all night. We could watch a movie. Want to pick something?"

Chick flick or action movie? They were back to simple choices. Safe, solid ground. Decisions she could handle, ones that didn't push too far, too fast.

"Sure." Georgia secured her towel. "There's a new Ryan Gosling movie that just released on DVD. It is probably on pay-per-view too."

He winced, but nodded in agreement. "Sounds good."

"It's based on a romance novel," she added.

"OK." He turned and punched a code into the lock on the door. It beeped twice and the door unlocked. Reaching inside, he turned on the light.

"You seriously want to watch a tear-jerking romance movie?" she asked, moving toward the open doorway. She knew he'd choose action/adventure any day.

"Georgia, I've barely slept this past week. Chances are I'm going to crash within the first five minutes. So pick whatever you want."

She smiled and walked past him into the condo. "Ryan Gosling, here we come."

Thirty minutes later, Eric joined her on the brown leather couch in front of the big-screen television. He'd changed into a white undershirt and flannel pajama pants that hung low on his hips, offering a glimpse of his chiseled stomach. And he'd selected a can of beer from the fridge.

"I see you found ice cream," he said, nodding at the carton in her hand.

She licked her spoon clean. "You can't watch a chick flick without chocolate."

"I'll take your word for it." Eric cracked open his beer can and took a long drink.

On the screen, Ryan Gosling stripped off his shirt. Eric wrapped his arm around her and drew her close. Sitting here with him, her body buzzing with physical delight from their visit to the hot tub, eating ice cream and watching a movie—this felt simple and fun. The emotional rush she'd felt earlier when he'd held her? She'd locked that outside.

For now. She suspected it wouldn't stay there.

They watched in silence for a while. Eric finished his beer and set the can aside, still holding her tight. On the screen, Mr. Gosling remained topless. It didn't seem to matter what he was doing, the producers had clearly decided their male star should remain partially dressed for the duration of the film.

"If I'd known I'd be watching you stare at a half-naked Ryan whatever-his-name all night, I would have insisted on the new Bond movie," Eric mumbled.

She would have probably liked that more too. But she didn't want Eric looking at her and wondering if the violence on the screen would trigger a bad memory. She'd rather joke about ice cream and movie stars while pressed against his warm body.

"You don't think he's cute?" she asked.

No answer. She glanced at the man next to her. Head back, mouth open, and eyes closed, Eric had passed out.

Georgia turned her attention back to the screen. Maybe she'd watch the Bond movie after this ended. A few more hours curled up next to Eric, his hand heavy on her shoulder, sounded better than tossing and turning in his spare bedroom, pretending to sleep.

And this time, it wouldn't be her fear of nightmares keeping her up. She knew that in the morning, all of this, the hot tub sex and cuddling on the couch, would end. By the time the sun came up, she needed to accept the fact that holding on to her heart was not the same as taking the coward's way out. She had what she wanted—one wild night with Eric. That had to be enough.

Chapter Nine

ERIC WOKE UP to sunlight pouring into the condo's open living area. He'd slept on the couch. At some point, he'd shifted from sitting to lying down. And someone—Georgia—had thrown a blanket over him.

Sitting up, he glanced around. No sign of her.

He moved to the kitchen and found a hot pot of coffee. He poured a cup and headed for the door. From the deck, he spotted her at the ocean's edge wearing the same bathing suit she'd lost in his pond last weekend. The waves crashed around her thighs. The water had to be freezing, but she didn't seem to care. She walked in, waited for a wave, and dove under.

"Crazy," he murmured. But it wasn't just the early morning dip in the Pacific that bothered him. The way she approached life, as if it was one big thrill ride, made him wonder about last night. Between the wild game of truth or dare and the way she'd insisted they remain outside, in full view, made him wonder, did she want him or just another rush?

He couldn't push that question away, not anymore. This thing between them was turning into more than stolen kisses. They needed to take the next step and tell her brother. Liam deserved to hear the facts from them, not rumors or hearsay.

Eric followed her movements in the surf. In a few minutes, she'd be freezing. Scanning the sand for a towel, he came up empty. He set his coffee on the hot tub lid, grabbed one, and headed for the stairs.

Georgia emerged, dripping wet, when he reached the water's edge. "Playing lifeguard?"

"Someone has to keep you safe." He draped the towel over her shoulders, but stopped short of wrapping it around her front. Instead, he used it like a net, drawing her toward him.

"I'm a strong swimmer," she said, stepping close.

She took the edge of the towel from him and reached her arms up, cocooning them from prying eyes. Eric looked up and down the shore. A couple walked in the distance, and in the other direction, a woman with her dog ran down the shore.

"What if you got caught in the undertow?" He ran his hand up her arm, to the back of her neck.

"If you came in to get me, it would pull you under too."

"It might. Or I might save you." He toyed with the string at the back of her neck. One quick tug and it came undone. The fabric fell away from her breasts. His hands covered her, pressing against her tight nipples. Leaning forward, he whispered in her ear, "Admit it. One day, you might need me."

"To rescue me? Never."

Her expression was a mix of defiance and desire. He lowered his forehead to hers. "*Rescue* and *need* aren't the same."

He ran his hands over the curve of her waist. Holding her hip with one hand, he slipped the other beneath her bikini bottom, caressing her soft, wet folds.

"Careful," she gasped. "We're still on the beach."

"Let's go inside."

Tension rippled through her. She stepped away, drawing the towel tight around her body, forcing him to release his intimate hold on her.

"Georgia?" He felt the moment breaking apart. And he had a sinking feeling that there wasn't a damn thing he could do about it.

His phone vibrated against his leg. Eric pulled it out, checked the screen, and glanced at her. He wanted to find out what she was thinking right now. But—

"I need to take this."

Eric stepped away, holding the phone to his ear. "Craig," he greeted the crew chief filling in for Liam, who was taking a much-needed break after last week's fire. "Is there a problem?"

"The guys from B&B Trucking never showed. I have the crew here at White Rock, ready to load the timber from the fire line we cut, but no trucks."

"I'll make some calls." He lowered the phone and turned to Georgia. "I have to do some work before we head out to pick up Nate. See if I can find a new trucking company on a Sunday."

She walked beside him as they headed for the stairs, close but not touching. "You could call Summers Family Trucking."

"Katie's brothers." Eric nodded. "Not a bad idea. They're smaller than B&B, but could probably handle this job."

They reached the gate to his deck, and Eric punched in the code. He glanced over at Georgia. Wrapped in the large towel and shaking from her cold morning swim, she looked small and fragile. He fought the urge to scoop her up, carry her inside, and warm her in the shower.

He held the gate, allowing her to walk past him. Work needed him, but that wasn't the only thing holding him back. She'd pulled away from him. He wanted to know why, but he didn't want to push.

Stepping inside the condo, Eric placed his hand on her shoulder and gave a light squeeze. "Are you OK?"

She nodded, moving out of his grasp. "Just cold."

It was more than that, but he let it go for now.

AN HOUR LATER, Georgia watched the condo slip out of sight as they pulled onto the main street, leaving the coast behind. Eric sat in the driver's seat, calmly focused on the road. The space felt cramped, as if his presence shrunk the otherwise spacious interior, barely leaving room for her to think. And every time she glanced over and saw his hands deftly manning the wheel or adjusting the A/C, she thought of how his fingers had felt on her skin last night.

"Did you resolve the trucking problem?" she asked, trying to focus on the scenery.

"Yeah. The Summers brothers stepped up," he said. "It looks like we'll be using them more and more. Liam won't be too happy about it though. They don't exactly get along." He glanced over at her. "Speaking of your brother, I think we should sit down with Liam. Tell him about us."

"Eric," she said slowly. She'd been thinking about how to tell him she couldn't repeat last night. And he'd given her the perfect out. "I don't want one night of sex to come between you and my brother."

"This doesn't end here, Georgia."

She kept her eyes fixed on the pavement in front of them. "Yes, it does."

"Georgia, you asked me last night what I was most afraid of."

"It was just a game, Eric."

"No," he said, slowing as the road curved. His grip tightened on the steering wheel. "This is more. Can't you see that? I've wanted you for so long it feels criminal."

Not much blindsided her. Not anymore. She made sure of it. But hearing those words? From Eric?

"How long?" She tried to keep her voice light and firm, but it wavered.

"Remember your junior year of high school when you went to prom with that football player and stayed out all night?"

She nodded. "I was grounded for the rest of the year. I remember."

"Liam told me about that and I lost it. I drove all night, planning to come home and beat the kid up so he never laid a hand on you again."

Georgia bit her lip. He'd wanted her since junior year? No, it wasn't possible. She'd tried to catch his attention, insisting Liam let her tag along whenever he was going places with Eric. But Eric had always treated her like a friend.

"What stopped you?" she asked.

"I saw you first. You were so happy despite the grounding that I couldn't do it. So I drove back to school and buried my jealousy."

Her eyebrows shot up. "You were jealous of Tommy Lewis? I had a better orgasm the other night, on your bed, than I ever had with him."

"Not sure I wanted to know that," he murmured. "And I think you have yourself to thank for that."

"No. It was you," she said softly, focusing on the trees speeding by outside the window. "It's always been you. Even back when it was criminal."

"Then let's do this right"—his tone was firm—"and tell Liam."

"No."

She heard the rush of the road outside, but Eric remained silent. Still, his tension radiated through the car.

"What's holding you back, Georgia?" he asked finally. "What are you afraid of when it comes to us?"

Georgia closed her eyes, her hands clenched tight in her lap. She felt as if she were out in the open surrounded by the unknown, and he was asking her to remove her body armor. If she set aside her defenses, if she let him in, what would keep her strong?

"I'm not ready," she said evenly. "I'm just not."

Out of the corner of her eye, she saw his hands tighten on the steering wheel. "OK. I won't tell him. You have my word."

"Thank you."

"But Georgia, don't walk away from us. We could make this work. Trust me."

She nodded. But in her head, the questions swirled. How could they move forward when he wanted more than she could give? Talking to Liam implied a future for them. A relationship bound with commitment and promises. She couldn't travel down that path, not when her emotions were off the table. Georgia knew she should tell him. But she hated the idea that he'd see it as a problem that needed fixing, the same way he'd stepped up and offered her a job when her brother asked. Or how he'd jumped in to keep her from hiking with a perfectly capable firefighter.

Georgia stared out the window as they turned off the highway and headed for his mother's house. Maybe that was the dead-end barrier they could not get past. How could she open up to someone who looked at her and saw her weaknesses, not her strengths?

Chapter Ten

ERIC HELD TIGHT to his frustration, knowing that if he let it loose, Georgia would bolt. But it took all his self-restraint not to punch his fist against the steering wheel. Georgia was slipping away, backpedaling out of his life as quickly as she'd walked in and dropped her towel.

He turned into his mother's drive and put the car in park. Nate waved from the front window as if he'd been waiting for Eric.

"Do you want me to go get him?" she asked.

"No." He opened the car door. "Wait here. I'll be right back."

He glanced over his shoulder as he raised his fist and knocked on his mother's door. Georgia was still there. But he wasn't so sure for how long.

"I should have listened to Liam," he murmured, raising his hand to knock again.

His best friend had told him over and over that Georgia wasn't equipped to handle a relationship right now. She had too much baggage. But Eric had let years of desire push that sad fact to the side. She'd said that she didn't need anyone to help her, but she was wrong. She'd been through too much to handle it on her own. Hell, if they had any hope of moving beyond one night in his hot tub, she had to open up and let him help her.

"Eric." His mother smiled, opening the door. "Come in."

"Hi, Mom." He leaned forward, kissing her cheek. "Georgia's waiting in the car. Is Nate ready?"

"He's packing his bag and saying good-bye to the puppies. They were born last night."

"That's great," he said, knowing he'd hear about little else from Nate on the drive home.

"Please come inside," she said. "I need to talk to you before you go."

He shifted his weight but didn't step inside. "Not today. I have to get home. I had a trucking problem this morning. I can't stay and chat today. Maybe next time."

His mother pressed her lips together. "We're moving at the end of the month. To Arizona. Henry went down last month to look at condos. We found an independent living community we like."

Eric froze. His mother was walking out his life again. Only this time, she wasn't leaving just him behind. His jaw clenched and his hands formed tight fists at his sides. "Did you tell Nate?"

"Not yet," she said. "I wanted to speak with you first. We didn't make the choices lightly. The dry air will be better for us. Henry's asthma is getting worse."

Henry. Of course. The man who'd been in her life for five minutes trumped the son she'd left behind countless times and the grandson still moving past his parents' tragic deaths.

"I'll talk to Nate," he said. "I'll handle it."

"I hope you'll come visit us once we're settled. We'll have a pool. I think Nate might enjoy it."

His nephew appeared in the doorway. Eric scooped him, holding him tight. "Hey, buddy. How are the puppies?"

Nate launched into a monologue as Eric carried him to the car and secured him in his car seat. Georgia kept the conversation flowing, asking questions about the dogs while Eric drove. An hour slipped by, and toward the end Nate fell asleep.

"It's his nap time," Georgia whispered.

Eric nodded, not trusting himself to say a word. His mother was picking up and moving away. Logically, he understood the reasons. But he couldn't push past how easy it was for her to say good-bye.

Eric turned into the drive. "I'll carry him inside and put him to bed."

But when they pulled up to the house, Eric spotted Liam's truck blocking the entrance to his garage. Georgia's brother leaned against the driver's side, his expression grim.

"Change of plan," Eric said. "You take Nate up, and I'll talk to Liam."

"Do you think he knows?" she asked.

"No. And I won't tell him. Not today." He'd had enough for one day. And right now, if Liam took a swing at him, which his friend would, Eric would fight back. Liam deserved to land a punch. Hell, maybe two. Eric had violated his trust and taken advantage of his sister. When the time came, Eric would take the hits without fighting back. But not today.

She opened her door as soon as he put the car in park.

"Georgia." Liam hugged her tight. "Doesn't he ever give you a day off?"

"Eric is just doing his part to keep me out of trouble," she said, her voice light and teasing. "Are you checking up on me again?"

"Wish I was." Liam released Georgia and looked at Eric. "I saw Caroline Smith last night."

Eric gently lifted Nate out of his car seat. "The regional director for the Oregon Department of Forestry?"

Liam nodded. "She had some interesting things to say."

Shit, Eric didn't have room in his head for another crisis. Not right now. "Come inside. We'll grab a beer, and you can tell me."

"While you two gossip, I'll be inside putting Nate to bed," Georgia said, taking the sleeping three-year-old from him.

"I'll let you in." Eric headed for the house, unlocking the door and holding it for Georgia. Liam followed close behind.

After she disappeared up the stairs, Eric led his friend to the kitchen. "What did Caroline Smith say?"

"The DOF is starting an investigation into the White Rock fire," Liam said.

Eric ran his hands through his hair. "Not good news, but that's their job. I was expected to cover my share, maybe more, of the cost to put the fire out. It was my land and my operation."

"I got the sense they're digging for more," Liam said. "The good news is Caroline likes you."

"The feeling isn't mutual." He opened the fridge and pulled out two bottles.

"I was thinking maybe you could take her to dinner." Liam accepted the beer, twisting off the cap with his hand. "A couple of nights with her wouldn't kill you. Might soften her up."

"You came over here to set Eric up on a date?" Georgia walked into the kitchen. She glanced at Eric. "Nate's in bed and sound asleep."

"Good," Eric said to Georgia before turning back to her brother. "And no, I'm not taking Caroline Smith to dinner. We'll handle this through proper channels on Monday morning. We filed the correct paperwork and observed the regulations. We have nothing to hide, and we're willing to pay what we owe."

"Handle what?" Georgia asked.

Eric gave her a quick rundown of Liam's not-so-good news. Her eyes widened as she listened.

"First the fire and now this. Liam, we're not going to let you visit if you keep showing up with these doom-and-gloom reports."

"Hey, I'm just the messenger, passing on what I heard," Liam said, raising his hands in protest. "And Caroline wasn't the only person I ran into last night. Chad Summers was at the bar. He was drunk and we got into it a bit. Before he left, Chad said Katie's been hanging around here."

"Babysitting. Georgia needed a night off," Eric said quickly. The last thing he needed was Liam wondering if Eric was fooling around with Katie. He wasn't sure if that was better or worse than telling his friend he'd been with his sister.

Liam nodded, turning to Georgia. "So what did you do on your night out? Hot date?"

"Very," Georgia said.

Eric choked on his beer, covering it with a cough. So much for a discreet babysitter. And if the Summers brothers were talking, others in town would soon be too. There was no such thing as a secret in a small town. They needed to tell Liam. Soon.

He glanced at Georgia, but she was too busy staring her brother down.

Liam frowned, his grip tightening on his beer. "Who is he?"

"I don't kiss and tell," Georgia said with a smile.

And great, she was enjoying this, pushing her brother's buttons. But Eric could tell from Liam's stern expression, he didn't find her game funny.

"Look, Georgie." Liam spoke softly, but there were undercurrents of steel in his tone as he used her childhood nickname. "Eric and I have been talking, and we don't think you're ready to date. I don't want some jerk taking advantage of you."

"You've been talking to Eric about my love life behind my back?" Eric heard the warning in her voice. She wasn't finding this amusing. Not anymore. But Liam appeared oblivious.

"We're worried about you. You've only been back a few months. You need time to adjust," her brother said. "So who is he?"

Georgia cocked her head. "What will you do if I tell you?"

"Have a conversation with him," Liam said flatly.

"With your fists?"

Liam's jaw tightened as if he was grinding his teeth. "If necessary. Has he done something that would make me want to hit him?"

Yes, Eric thought, closing his eyes and picturing Georgia in his hot tub.

"No," she said. "But if he does, I'll handle it. I'm a big girl, Liam. No one is going to take advantage of me. I can take care of myself. And I'm more than capable of choosing whom to date, which I'm sure you'll be glad to hear is a big fat no one right now."

"But—"

"Ask Eric," she added. "I was with him the night Katie stayed with Nate."

Liam turned and Eric braced for a punch. Part of him would welcome it because shit, he wanted Georgia's words, *big fat no one*, to be a lie. He wanted her to be his. And he wanted to do this right, come clean to his friend and make her a part of his life.

"We went four-wheeling," Georgia continued. "I've been a little stir-crazy, and since you two don't approve of me running off to do things on my own, I brought Eric along."

Eric nodded. He hated lying to his friend, but he'd promised Georgia. And if he wanted her trust, he couldn't break his word.

Liam came over, resting his hand on Eric's shoulder. "Thanks for looking out for her."

"Always," Eric said, looking straight at Georgia, hoping she heard the truth in that one word. "Always."

"And last night, he took me to the coast," Georgia added.

Eric frowned at her. Liam wasn't an idiot. If she kept pressing, he'd put the pieces of the puzzle together. And connecting the dots was no way for Liam to find out.

"But don't worry, big brother," she continued. "We stayed in and watched the new Ryan Gosling movie. Nothing too exciting."

Liam snorted. "Man, I owe you one for that."

Eric looked over at Georgia. She was still smiling, but it looked forced.

"I'm going to take a nap," Georgia said. "I'll leave you boys to your gossip."

Eric watched her leave, knowing that was a lie. Georgia didn't sleep much. Even when he worked late, she was up when he got home most nights. After Liam left, he should swing by her room and talk. Or maybe he should let her have some time and space to think things through. He should probably do that himself. Between Georgia, his mother, and now the DOF investigation, it was a wonder his head hadn't exploded.

Chapter Eleven

WHEN KATIE HAD invited her out for a new homecoming adventure, Georgia had jumped at the chance for a distraction from the constant stream of questions and doubts running through her mind about her time at Eric's condo. Georgia had expected a trail ride or a hike. But no, her friend had driven her straight to Ariel's Hair & Nail Salon.

"Waiting for nail polish to dry is not exactly my idea of a fun morning." Georgia wiggled her freshly painted red toes. The color was bright and cheerful, but did little for her brooding mood.

"Sit back and relax," Katie said. "Drink your lemon water. This is girl time. You need this. And now that we're alone, I want all the details."

After their pedicures, they'd moved to the salon's back patio to sip the supposedly detoxifying water and wait for their nails to dry.

"I don't kiss and tell," Georgia said, hoping the line she'd used with her brother last night would work on Katie.

"Fair enough. But I have one question. If your brother knew, would he start throwing punches?"

"Yes."

Katie let out a sigh, covering her heart with her hand.

"Oh please, this is not a fairy-tale romance," Georgia said. "And I have a question for you. How did your brother find out you were watching Nate the other night?"

Katie's eyes widened. "Not from me."

"Chad told Liam that I'm seeing someone. And Liam confronted me last night. In front of Eric."

Katie closed her eyes. "Oh no. I mentioned that I'd been playing trains with Nate to Lila. The receptionist at the office," she said, referring to her family trucking company. "She has a two-year-old boy who is just starting to like trains. She must have said something. I'm sorry."

"It's OK," Georgia said. "I told him Eric was helping me find an outlet for my adventurous spirit."

Katie laughed. "There's a degree of truth to that. Do you think Liam suspects something more?"

"Maybe." Georgia stared at her red toes. "But it doesn't matter. It's over."

"Because of Liam?" Katie picked up the pitcher of lemon water and refilled their glasses.

"Yes. But only a little."

"You're entitled to your private life," Katie said, her voice strong and fierce. "You and Eric—that has nothing to do with Liam. Don't let your brother stand in your way."

"It's complicated." Her fear of opening up and letting someone in, leaning on them and trusting them, ran bone deep. She could see that now.

Katie reached over and took her hand. "Honey, you've loved Eric Moore since you were a teenager. This was never simple. But if neither one of you is willing to make the first move, to push this further, then you're at a standstill. And I'm starting to think that would hurt you more than anything."

Georgia nodded, the truth in her friend's words sinking in. "He made the first move. He wanted to tell my brother. I'm the one holding back."

"Oh, Georgia. Why?"

Georgia stared at the mountains. She was home. Safe. Yet, it still felt as if she couldn't let down her guard, as if she needed to fight her way through every minute of every single day. And she had to do it by herself.

"I get the feeling he wants to step into my life and take over," she said. "And he wants promises, ones I don't think I can make without cutting away at my independence."

It might not happen overnight, but over time, she had a feeling that letting him in, opening her heart to him, would weaken her.

Katie gave her hand a squeeze. "Talk to Eric. Explain how you feel. I think he might surprise you."

HOURS LATER, GEORGIA closed the door to Nate's room without making a sound. The little boy had protested going to bed without seeing Eric, but she'd insisted. She'd waited as long as she could, and Nate had nearly fallen asleep on the floor beside his train tracks.

She headed for the kitchen, mentally switching gears from toddlers and trains to how she would approach her conversation with Eric tonight. Exposing her emotional vulnerability—it was exactly what she'd been trying to avoid that first night when she'd gone into his bedroom. But if she didn't, Katie was right—they'd reach a standstill. And that's the one thing Georgia could not stomach—hiding from her life, instead of taking action. She had to face her fears. This was her life. She had to live it, even if doing so hurt.

She went to the kitchen and started cleaning the dinner dishes, scraping the remains of Nate's mac and cheese into the trash. In her pocket, her cell vibrated.

"I'm at home, Liam," Georgia said, holding her phone against her ear with her shoulder while she finished loading the dishwasher. "I just put Nate to bed, and I'm getting ready to prepare his snack for preschool tomorrow. Nothing crazy."

Unless you include preparing to confront my lover, who also happens to be your best friend.

"I'm not calling to check up on you," her brother said. "Not this time. I wanted to give you a heads-up that Eric had a bad day."

Georgia frowned. "Worse than fighting a forest fire?"

"Yeah. This morning he had to fire B&B Trucking. Their guys showed up late again. The owner didn't take it well. He'd been working with Moore Timber since Eric's father ran the business. Summers Family Trucking stepped up. But as soon as we fixed that problem, he got called into a DOF meeting. His assistant told me he left in a huff," her brother said. "So go easy on him tonight."

"I will." And that meant the little talk she'd planned would have to wait.

"No wild stunts," Liam added.

"I'll call and cancel my BASE jumping plans."

"Georgia—"

"Good night, Liam." She hung up the phone and opened the fridge. The housekeeper had left a pot of chicken stew and wild rice. Healthy, but not exactly comfort food. Georgia pulled out the weekend bacon and began heating a pan. She had just started slicing the tomato when Eric opened the door leading to the attached garage.

Her senses turned up to high alert before she even caught sight of him. And when she looked up?

It didn't matter what he wore, he couldn't hide his drool-worthy muscles. But tonight, seeing him in his business suit? Her fingers itched to unbutton his dress shirt and explore what lie beneath. Her gaze traveled up his torso to his face, noting the lines of exhaustion around his eyes and the tightness in his jaw. Poor man, he looked as if the past twenty-four hours had drained him completely.

"I'm making BLTs," she said, turning her attention back to the tomato before she sliced her fingers.

"I smelled the bacon in the garage." His voice was a deep rumble. "I thought I was on restriction."

She started assembling the sandwiches, trying not to think about the way her breasts perked up at the sound of his voice. They needed to talk tonight before she even considered going down that road. "Liam called. Said you had a bad day. Why don't you sit down and I'll grab you a drink. Beer?"

"Water is fine." He shrugged off his jacket and loosened his tie, undoing the top button of his dress shirt before sinking into a chair.

Georgia brought the sandwiches to the table and sat across from him. "Do you want to talk about it?" she asked.

"Bad day. That's all." Eric shook head. "The DOF believes we failed to follow the fire precautions. They're accusing us of running chainsaws during restricted hours."

Her eyes widened. "But you didn't, right?"

"I sure as hell hope not. We'd be on the hook for the full cost of the fire if we did," he said. "But it's not the money that gets to me. I hate sitting in those meetings, answering their damn questions, when I know they're fishing for some way to pin this on us. They won't have cold, hard facts until they determine the fire's point of origin. I just want to forget about it until then."

Freeze the feelings, the weight of it all, and set it aside. She understood that better than most. "If you need an escape, we could skinny-dip in the pond after dinner. The cold water always makes me feel better."

Eric set down his sandwich, shaking his head. "I don't think an adrenaline rush will solve my problems."

"I wasn't suggesting a rush—"

"This investigation has real consequences, Georgia. For my company and for your brother."

The spark of irritation she'd felt yesterday when Liam demanded to know the details of her personal life as if she were a teenager who couldn't be trusted returned. "I know all about real consequences."

"I know, Georgia," he said with a sigh. "But this problem can't be solved by jumping into cold water or with kinky sex."

And neither could hers. She knew that despite her attempts to bury her emotions. She understood what she was feeling, and the fears that pushed her to make the choices she did, far better than Eric or her brother gave her credit for. They pretended they knew better, but they didn't have a clue what she'd been through.

Because she hadn't told them. She hadn't trusted them or herself enough to share those experiences. That was on her. If she wanted them to see her strength, to understand, she had to open up.

"The other day in your bedroom or Saturday night, in the hot tub, it wasn't about chasing the next rush. I had sex with you because I wanted you too much to walk away," she said, her voice firm. "But you're right. My experience overseas left me with this need to feel alive. It's the only way I know how to keep going. There are days, less now than before, when I wake up amazed I'm still here. Why me? Of all the people who served alongside me, why did I live? And what am I doing now to prove I deserve a chance to move on when so many others didn't?"

"Georgia, I'm sorry. You were right. I had a bad day. I should not have snapped at you," he said quietly. "You don't have to talk about this."

"These memories and feelings follow me around, and I keep wondering when I'll find the words, when I'm going to trust someone enough to let them in. And if anyone will be there to listen when I do."

She saw the concern in his eyes. Tonight was not the night for this conversation. She knew that. But if not now, when?

"I'm here," he said, his words strong and firm as he leaned back in his chair. "I'm listening."

"The men and women I served with, they were good people. Mitch had a wife and a kid back home in North Carolina. Jennifer had twin girls at home. Those kids were her world, and she wanted them to be proud of her. Louis, he was raised by his grandmother and talked about her like she was a saint. They were all such good people. And then..."

Georgia closed her eyes. "The first time, I was traveling in a three-vehicle convoy. Mortar rounds exploded one right after the other. Louis, the gunner I was riding with, he was hit. Our vehicle was on fire. We had to get out, but Louis was unresponsive. I had to pull him out."

She heard the sound of Eric's chair moving across the floor, but she kept her eyes closed. She suspected he'd walked around the table, as she felt him at her side, but he didn't touch her.

"One minute Louis was telling me about his grandmother's cooking," she continued. "The next I'm dragging his body out of a burning vehicle. I didn't know we'd lost him. I thought he still had a chance. I rode with him, with his body, to the hospital after the firefight ended. But he was already gone."

"Georgia, honey—"

"The people I met," she continued, unable to stop now that she'd started to recount her experiences, "men and women I worked with, shared meals with, they were killed over there. Mortar attacks, IED blasts..."

Georgia opened her eyes and looked up at Eric, seeing the mounting worry in his blue eyes. "I know all about real consequences."

The pity on his face sliced through her, cutting deep. She could handle so much, but not blatant sympathy.

"Don't look at me like that." She pushed back from the table and stood, facing him.

He shook his head. "I'm just so damn sorry you had to go through that."

"I'm not," she said honestly. And maybe that was the piece of the puzzle no one understood. They wanted to shield her from the memories, while she wanted to face them head-on. She wanted to live, truly *live* as if each breath mattered, without forgetting.

"I don't regret serving my country," she said. "We did great work over there. I served alongside people who believed so strongly in our mission, who believed in what our country stands for, in our freedoms. It was an honor. And to return alive—that's a gift. One I try every day to feel worthy of. I can't do that if I'm drowning in grief. So I push back against anything that makes me feel too much. Including you. I want to let you in, believe me I do. But

I've been so afraid to open up when it feels like there is so little holding me together sometimes."

"You don't need to be afraid." He reached out, running his hand down the side of her face. "And you don't have to be worthy. You just have to be yourself. Who you are—that's enough, Georgia."

She turned her head away from his touch. Through the sliding glass doors, she stared out into the dark night. It was as if she'd slammed her fist down on the button labeled Emotions, the one she'd been so afraid to touch. And it had left her more exposed, more vulnerable, than when she'd stripped down and climbed into bed with him.

She crossed her arms tightly in front of her chest. It was funny how something as simple as sharing a memory could upend her world. Maybe she should have kept her mouth shut. He'd had a bad day. He didn't need this tonight. And she had a sinking feeling she didn't either. It was one thing to imagine the conversation while waiting for her toenails to dry and another to say the words.

Georgia looked back at Eric. God, she wished she could backtrack to the beginning of this conversation and start over. He probably did too.

She shook her head, her fingers pressing tight against her sides. "I bet you're wishing you'd chosen to go skinny-dipping in the pond when you had the chance."

Chapter Twelve

ERIC STARED DOWN at this woman he'd known his entire life. He'd misjudged her. Her wild actions were a shield to protect her from feeling too much, too soon. Georgia had survived a type of hell he could barely imagine, pulling her friend's body from a burning vehicle. How did a person move past that and return to day-to-day life? He didn't know. He had a feeling nobody did. But she was doing it. Her so-called rushes were a defense mechanism, a way of coping while she gave herself time to heal.

Just like her words.

I bet you're wishing you'd chosen to go skinny-dipping in the pond when you had the chance.

No. He'd gladly face another grueling day discussing the hows and whys surrounding a forest fire, if it meant Georgia would open up to him about the one part of her life he knew so little about. He'd been waiting for her to let him in and trust that he could help her.

But he had a feeling she'd reached her limit. Maybe right now, freezing her memories in the cold water of his pond was exactly what she needed.

"Let's do it now," he said.

"Do what?"

"Swim in the pond. Right now."

"Eric."

He placed his index finger under her chin, lifting it slightly. "I dare you."

She smiled and he sensed her relief. This was what she needed right now. They could talk about her memories later. Tonight, tomorrow, whenever she wanted to, he'd be there to listen. "I'll grab Nate's monitor," she said. "You get the towels."

Georgia stepped back, pulling her T-shirt over her head and tossing it on the table beside their abandoned meal. She plucked the monitor off the counter. Eric unbuttoned his dress shirt as he moved to the door leading to the garage. He opened it, reaching inside for the stacks of towels kept on a shelf. Then he followed her out into the night.

Stepping over her discarded shorts, he headed for the dock. A full moon illuminated the outline of Georgia's naked body standing on the dock's edge, poised to dive. He stopped in the grass, memorizing the slope of her curves. She'd never looked more perfect than she did at this moment with her naked body on the verge of movement under the Oregon night sky.

A second later, she disappeared into the water. Eric broke into a run. Dropping the towels on the docks, he stripped off the rest of his clothes before following her into the pond. The cold shocked his senses at first, so different from the late summer night air, but as he swam along the surface toward Georgia, his body adjusted.

"Feel better?" he asked, capturing her in his arms. With her body pressed against his chest, he leaned back, using the water for support as they drifted toward the shore.

"Yes."

With her back to his front, he couldn't see her face. But she felt relaxed in his arms.

"And you?" she asked.

"Georgia, I felt better the moment I saw you tonight," he said. "But now that I have you here, naked in my arms, I feel pretty damn good."

She broke free from his hold and turned. "How good?"

Grabbing her hand, he used two powerful kicks to push through the water until they reached a place where he could stand. She swam willingly into his embrace, wrapping her legs around his waist, her arms looping around his neck.

Unlike the first night on his bed or the time at his condo, she felt completely free with him and her desires. Whatever had been holding her back, those fears she'd mentioned earlier, which were closely bound to her time at war, weren't here now.

Despite the cool water, Eric's body responded to the feel of her against him. And so did his heart. He'd done a lot of good and right things in his life. But he'd never helped someone by simply listening.

Holding her head in his hands, he kissed her, thoroughly and deeply. For the first time since she'd plunged their friendship into new waters, he explored her. She wasn't just the girl he'd had a crush on for years. Georgia was a brave, resilient woman. He'd thought she needed him, but he was beginning to suspect it was the other way around.

She drew back, breaking their kiss. "You're shaking."

"You are too," he said, smiling. "The water is fucking cold."

She moved, her breasts rubbing against his chest, her legs tightening around his middle.

"That's the whole point," she said. "The cold water, it's supposed to be a rush, remember?"

"Yeah. I'm feeling it alright." He turned and started walking to the shore, still holding her body tight against him, craving the contact as much as the warmth. "But I think it's time to get out."

On the dock, he reluctantly set her down and picked up a towel. He wrapped it around her, rubbing her arms to warm her up. He looked down at her chest. "You're cold."

"No."

The towel slipped through his fingers, falling to the dock.

Georgia looked up at him, watching and waiting. But he didn't touch her. He wanted her, so damn much, but there were things he needed to tell her, about Liam, the investigation—

"Close your eyes," she said softly.

"Georgia—"

"Shh." She pressed her finger against his lips, silencing him. "This might surprise you, but I have a long list of things I want to do to you too. Please close your eyes."

This time, he honored her request. The second he did, he felt her fingertips on his shoulders. He swallowed a gasp. The other night, he'd been the one doing the touching and exploring. But he wasn't going to deny the fact that he liked having the tables turned.

He felt her shift close, her breath tickling his ear.

"Push your responsibilities aside. Just enjoy the moment," she said. "Easier said than done. Believe me, I know. But try. Trust me. Tonight, I've got you."

Her lips brushed the skin behind his ear. And then the feel of her body hovering close to his, her mouth on him, vanished. He was tempted to open his eyes.

"Keep them closed," she said. Her voice sounded lower. The grass at his feet rustled, and a fully formed picture of what was happening, what she planned to do, filled his mind.

"Georgia." Her name on his lips was a plea to both keep going and stop.

Her hands wrapped around him, running up and down his dick. He moaned.

"I haven't reached the good part yet." He felt the words on the skin her hands continued to caress, up and down. One hand fell away, wrapping around his body, holding him close. Her tongue licked away the moisture slipping out the tip of his erection.

Eric opened his eyes and stared up at the stars. Her lips surrounded him, taking him so damn deep. He felt the sides of her hollow cheeks.

"Georgia." He laced his fingers through her hair, drawing her down farther. His hips thrust forward, demanding control as he set the rhythm. She didn't pull back.

"Georgia, stop me if this is too much," he managed through clenched teeth.

She dug her fingers into his ass. She wasn't letting go. Knowing she wanted this, shit, that turned him on.

One, two, three. He counted the stars, trying to hold off. He made it to five.

"I'm going to come." He released her head, waiting for her to pull back. But she didn't. Eric closed his eyes and let the orgasm wash over him. Right here, right now, it was pretty damn easy to follow her advice and live in the moment.

Slowly, Georgia let him go. He offered his hand, pulling her up and into his arms.

"I've wanted to do that for a long time," she said, tracing small circles on his chest.

"I have to admit, I'm hard-pressed to find a reason we waited so long."

"There's a long list," she said softly, her smile fading. "Trust me."

Shit, he knew he'd brought those reasons to the forefront of her mind. And his.

Eric stepped back, gently releasing her. He picked up the second towel, securing it around his waist, watching as she did the same. Wrapping his arm around her shoulders, Eric drew her against his side and headed up the hill to the house, stopping to retrieve the monitor.

"I want you to spend the night with me," he said. "In my bed."

"Yes."

Eric exhaled and relief seeped in. Deep down, he'd been afraid she'd retreat to her own room, pushing him away again. "Good."

She pressed in closer, as if she craved the feel of his body. "And tomorrow, I think we should tell Liam."

Eric hesitated. Earlier, in the kitchen, she hadn't given him a chance to explain the very real consequences of the DOF's investigation. They had accused the person calling the shots on the White Rock job site of running chainsaws after the restricted hours. Liam. Georgia's brother had been on-site harvesting those trees. Liam had been aware of the fire restrictions and told Eric he planned to run the equipment until one in the afternoon. But if he'd gone over, even by a few minutes…

Moore Timber could afford the fine. He kept a reserve for such occasions because forest fires were always a threat. But the financial cost was only one piece of the puzzle. If the DOF determined they'd violated the fire precautions, Eric would be forced to let Liam go. It didn't matter that he was Eric's best friend. Georgia's brother couldn't harvest trees for Moore Timber if he broke the rules. Not if his actions when out in the field threatened lives.

Georgia slipped out of his grasp as they entered the house. He knew he should tell her about Liam and the investigation. But not now. Tonight had been hard on her, telling him about her time in Afghanistan. He didn't want her worrying about her brother.

"We'll tell him soon," he promised.

Eric hoped like hell the DOF investigators were wrong. But until he knew for certain what happened the day the fire started, he couldn't tell Liam about his relationship with Georgia. Eric couldn't face telling his best friend that he'd violated his trust and slept with his sister, and then fire him.

Chapter Thirteen

GEORGIA STEPPED INTO Eric's room and closed the door, blocking out the rest of the world. She'd been here before, standing in front of his bed wrapped in a towel, her body wound tight with need. But tonight, she was going after what she wanted, knowing there was no end in sight.

"Eric, look at me."

He set the monitor on the bedside table and turned to her. Wearing a towel like some men wore kilts, low around his hips, highlighting the sculpted path down his stomach to what lie below, Eric stood with his feet apart and planted firmly on the floor. His hands moved to his waist as he watched and waited, following her orders.

"Watch my hands." Her fingers shaking, she tugged at her towel. It fell to the floor, pooling at her feet. Her fingers brushed her breasts, drawing soft, teasing circles.

"Georgia," he growled. He closed the space between them, tossing his towel aside, pulling her into his arms, and holding her tight against him.

"I thought you liked to watch," she teased.

"Not tonight. I need to touch you." He skimmed her low back, up her waist, and around to her front. He palmed her breasts, his hands caught between them. "But Christ, you're still shaking. You're cold."

She reached for him, holding him close. "Warm me up."

"I will." His hands moved to her shoulders while every part of her screamed, *touch me lower.* "But first, a hot shower."

He took her hand and led her into the attached master bath. He pulled a dry towel from the chrome bar with his free hand and draped it around her shoulders. He turned to the walk-in shower, opened the glass door, and adjusted the knobs. "It will take just a second to warm up."

Georgia looked around the room. When stationed overseas, she'd dreamed about having this much personal space. Not to bathe, but to live and sleep. It was easy to forget sometimes how far Eric had moved from the life they'd lived growing up. He'd always been a step above her on the economic scale, but she'd figured her happy home life with two loving, still-married-to-each-other parents evened the score. Or at least it had back then.

She ran her hand over the marble counter, devoid of clutter except for his razor and, at the far edge, a stack of magazines with a book on top. She scanned the title. *Soldiers with PTSD: A Case Study.*

She turned and found Eric an arm's length away, watching her, his lips pressed into a thin line.

"Attempting to figure me out?" She tried for a light and playful tone—and failed. The more she thought about Eric reading this book, the more she wanted to scream. She held the towel tight, as if it could keep her cries bottled inside.

"Liam gave it to me," he admitted without looking away.

"Have you read it?"

He held up his hands, palms out in a universal sign of surrender. "I want to understand, Georgia."

She looked down at the cover. Four different pictures, all men in dress uniform, stared back at her. "I don't think it is that simple. I have a hard time believing there is a textbook answer to how people cope with war. Everyone who serves and returns home has their own story and faces their own, very personal challenges."

He nodded. "Yeah, I'm starting to get that."

"Good." She released her white-knuckle grip on the towel, but didn't let it fall away.

"Georgia, for what it is worth, I'm sorry."

Steam from the shower filled the room, warming her skin. But the sincerity she saw in his blue eyes sparked a feeling of heat and need deep inside. He cared. It was there in his expression, in his actions. "For reading a book? You don't have to apologize for that."

"Georgia."

He reached for her as if he thought she might bolt, run away, and hide. Her fear lingered, refusing to dissolve because she'd offered him a glimpse into what haunted her, but she was done pulling away from him.

"The mirror's starting to fog up," she said. "I think the shower is trying to tell us something."

"What is it saying?" His fingertips brushed her cheek. He lowered his mouth to hers. This kiss—it was a gentle caress, so unlike the way he'd claimed her mouth in the pond. Her desire stirred, slowly smoldering, responding to him. And then he released her.

"I think it's inviting us in." She let the towel fall and took his hand, leading him to the glass door. She stepped inside. The warmth surrounded her, the steam hitting her first and then the spray from the shower.

Eric followed, pressing up against her. His erection rubbed her low back. Water ran between them, lubricating his movements as he flexed his hips, lightly thrusting back and forth, teasing and taunting.

"Reach your arms up." His hands captured hers, lifting them, positioning her palms against the wall. "Hold them there. Don't let go."

His fingers ran down to her shoulders. Georgia closed her eyes, losing herself in the sensations, his hands on her breasts, her stomach, and finally between her thighs, exploring, experimenting with movement and pressure. His touch warmed her from the inside while the water worked on the outside.

He slipped a finger inside her, his thumb working slow circles over her clit. She wanted to explode, craved the orgasm more than her next breath, but not here, like this.

"I'm warm now." She released the tile wall, turning to face him.

Eric raised an eyebrow. "Is the shower kicking us out?"

Georgia nodded as he turned the knobs. The water stopped. There was nothing between them. No place to bury her feelings. And this time, she didn't want to leave them behind.

Running her hands up his powerful arms, she rose on her tiptoes, interlacing her fingers at the back of his neck. "I'm ready for bed."

Palming her bottom, Eric lifted her. "Wrap your legs around me."

Georgia obeyed, running her mouth and tongue over his neck as he carried her into the bedroom. He laid her down on the bed. She kept her eyes open, watching as he pulled out the drawer in his nightstand and withdrew a condom. He covered himself and joined her on the bed, his body hovering over hers.

Holding his weight on his forearms, he stared down at her silently, searching her expression. What did he need? What was he looking for? Whatever it was, she hoped he found it. For the first time, she felt as if she were giving him everything she had to offer.

"Please, Eric," she whispered, "make love to me."

She reached between them, wrapping her hand around his erection, guiding him until the tip touched her entrance. She let go, moving her hands to his hips. Her fingers pressed against his skin as her body lifted, taking him in. She didn't look away.

"I need more," she pleaded.

"Me too, Georgia," he said softly. "Me too."

He moved—thrusting again and again in a relentless rhythm, pushing her closer and closer.

"Eric," she gasped.

"Now, Georgia," he demanded, his jaw tight. "Now."

The orgasm ripped through her. Above her, Eric tensed, holding himself still, deep inside her, finding his own release.

She clung to him, letting the emotions overwhelm her from head to toe. Her love for him swelled and fear followed, but this time she didn't retreat. She held tight, trusting he'd be there to catch her if she fell apart.

ERIC WOKE TO an empty bed, the smell of breakfast drifting through the closed door. His body felt refreshed, renewed by the potent combination of sex and sleep, but his mind spun in ten different directions—the DOF investigation, Liam, Nate, Georgia.

He stood and took a quick, cold shower, his body responding to the memory of Georgia standing there, wet and slick with her hands against the wall. She'd let him in, allowing him to touch and explore. But he didn't have time to remember.

He dressed and headed for the kitchen. Stepping through the archway, he focused on Georgia. She stood in front of the stove, shoveling eggs onto plates beside buttered toast. She wore her everyday uniform, jeans and a T-shirt. He read the words written across her chest. "Why Hug a Tree When You Can Hug a Logger?"

He wanted to draw her close, wrap his arms around her. Instead, he settled for leaning down and brushing a kiss over her lips, inhaling her sweet, freshly showered scent. And then he stepped back, knowing Nate would be down soon. Plus Eric had to get to work.

"Morning to you too." She smiled at him. "You look fancy today. You're probably the only logger in the county who owns a three-piece suit."

"Another meeting with the Department of Forestry today," he said. "I need to head out now. Can you take Nate to school?"

"Of course." She held out a plate. "Do you have time for breakfast first?"

He shook his head. "Tell Nate I'm sorry and I'll make it up to him this weekend. He'll be in bed by the time I get home tonight. You OK to work late again?"

"Sure." She moved to the table, setting the plate in front of Nate's booster chair. "I'll cancel my hot date."

Eric froze, his briefcase in hand. The pond. The shower. The look in her eyes as she came beneath him on his bed. The images paraded through his mind. She'd been right there with him, open, trusting, and completely his.

"I'm kidding, Eric," she said. "I don't have plans. No hot dates. Go kick butt in your meetings today. Don't worry about us. I'll take care of Nate. We'll be fine."

He nodded. "Thank you. If you're still up, maybe I'll see you tonight."

"You will," she said. "Count on it."

Eric headed for his car, trying to focus his thoughts on work. But Georgia's words, the soapy smell of her skin, and the mental picture of her smiling up at him, stayed with him as he drove down the drive and turned onto the main road.

Last night, Georgia had shared pieces of herself that she'd kept buried for the past few months. Her trust was like a living, breathing thing, right there beside them as she'd looked at the book Liam had given him, and then back at him. It had followed them into the shower, and into the bedroom.

But was that enough? Would it keep her from walking away?

Eric parked his car in front of the Department of Forestry building, mentally leaving his uncertainty at its side. Right now, he needed to focus on the investigation threatening his company and his best friend, and have faith Georgia would be waiting for him at the end of the day.

Chapter Fourteen

ERIC HEARD THE knock on his office door and lifted his head, glancing out the window. The last time he'd looked up the sun had been dipping behind the mountains. Now it had vanished. He'd been going over crew logs and paperwork ever since he'd left the meeting with Caroline Smith, the DOF director leading the investigation. If she'd been interested in a dinner date at some point, she wasn't today. She'd been 100 percent professional. Not that Eric had offered. He was following the straight and narrow when it came to their investigation. He wanted to find out what happened as much as they did. It was his land and his responsibility.

"Come in," he called.

Liam walked into the room, still dressed in his work clothes after pulling a long day in the field. Eric had assigned him to a BLM land harvest, but that was government property. Caroline Smith had pretty much told him to sideline Liam, especially when it came to Bureau of Land Management projects, until he was cleared of wrongdoing. She'd said *if*, but Eric wanted to believe it was a *when*.

"I got your message. What's up?" Liam said, pausing in the doorway.

Liam never seemed comfortable in the office. And Eric could relate. It was hard to transition from working outside to a clean, refined office space. When Eric came in from a job, he often felt out of place in his boots and work clothes.

"Want a water or a beer?" Eric asked, pushing back from his desk.

"Water's fine."

Eric went to the minifridge he kept in the corner of his office and pulled out two plastic bottles. Handing one to Liam, he sat in one of the two leather chairs on the other side of his desk. Liam took the other.

"I heard the DOF was rough on you yesterday," Liam said.

Eric nodded. "I met with Caroline again this morning. They received an anonymous tip that our crew was running the equipment and felling trees past one in the afternoon on the day the fire started. It was called in yesterday afternoon."

"Shit." Liam shook his head. "We weren't. You know that. I was pushing the crew to get as far as we could so we could focus on loading the trucks. I had the guys from B&B Trucking waiting. We started loading by twelve forty-five that day."

Eric nodded.

"It had to be the lightning that passed through the night before," Liam said, leaning forward, resting his forearms on his thighs.

"It didn't rain in the section you were cutting?"

"No." Liam's grip tightened on his water bottle.

"You walked the perimeter of the work site that morning, checking for signs of smoke before you fired up the equipment?" Eric asked. Caroline had poised a similar question that morning. If lightning started the fire, how did they not see the smoke?

"You know we did."

Eric sighed. "I wasn't there."

"Yes, damn it! I sent two guys out to check for signs of fire. They came back and we fired up the chainsaws and got to work." Liam's eyes narrowed, his expression fierce. "Do they have a point of origin yet?"

"Not yet. The DOF is working on it. They plan to share their findings in the next few days." Eric drew a deep breath. "Until then, I need to pull you off the BLM harvest. Craig can take over."

"What the fuck, man?" Liam leapt out of his chair, running one hand through his hair. "You don't believe me? I was born and raised here too. I remember what it feels like to walk away from everything you own not knowing if it will be there when you come back. I was ten the last time, but that's not something you forget."

"No, it's not." Eric understood the heartache that went hand in hand with fire. His mother often waited until the last minute before evacuating. He'd been terrified they wouldn't get out in time. His father, who understood the threat a forest fire posed, demanded full custody of him and his sister after the last time. His mother had agreed without a fight, quickly moving in with her latest boyfriend. Of course, it hadn't lasted long. His dad had passed them back as soon as he met someone new.

"Knowing I'm the reason another kid has to wonder if he'll lose everything, that is my worst nightmare," Liam said. "I'd do everything I can to prevent that from happening."

Eric hesitated. He believed Liam. But he had to remain objective. If it were any other employee, Eric would have sidelined him immediately pending the investigation.

Liam stopped in the center of the room. "I've been your best friend since first grade. I have always been one hundred percent honest with you."

Eric closed his eyes, the guilt like a lead weight in his stomach. "I know. And as your friend, I believe you. But the DOF doesn't want you working on government land until we've cleared this up."

Liam looked him straight in the eye. "I can't believe this!"

"I'm sorry," Eric said. "There's nothing I can do. We need to play ball with them until we know what happened."

Liam raised his hand, pointing his index finger at Eric. "Keep Georgia out of this. She doesn't need to worry about me and this shit. Not right now."

Eric nodded. "I won't say a word. But if I were you, I wouldn't be afraid of her finding out. She's stronger than you think."

"You can't tell her, Eric," Liam ground out. Eric knew his friend was barely keeping a leash on his anger. "Not about this. I want your word."

"You have it."

Liam stormed out, slamming the door to Eric's office. Running his hand over his face, Eric stood and returned to the other side of his desk. He wanted this mess behind them. Of course, it would disappear only if the investigators came back and absolved Moore Timber of wrongdoing. Even then, putting things right with Liam would take time. And after he told his best friend about his relationship with Georgia? It might take damn near forever.

Georgia. She was opening up to him. Now he had to keep this from her. But he had a feeling she'd understand. Her faith in him felt solid. It was something he could count on. But was it enough? Was she falling for him because her heart wouldn't have it any other way? That was why he was close to putting his friendship with Liam on the line. He couldn't walk away from what he felt for Georgia. She was *his*.

He'd always cared for her. But now it felt as if he were tumbling headfirst over a cliff. He'd made the first leap, but caught himself on a branch. If he let go, if he allowed himself to free-fall into this relationship, he needed to be sure she was right there with him, committed to today, tomorrow, and the day after that.

But he wondered if the woman who'd been running scared from her feelings up until last night could handle words like *long-term* and *serious*, or if they'd sound like a foreign language. Sharing her memories didn't change the fact that they'd happened. And it didn't make them go away.

Eric shut down his computer, and with it his concerns. It was close to eleven. If he left now, Georgia might still be awake. She'd said she'd wait up, but he hadn't anticipated working this late.

He locked up the office and headed for his car. Twenty minutes later, he pulled into the garage, cut the engine, and climbed out of his vehicle. Briefcase in one hand, he opened the back door.

"Nooo!"

Eric walked into the kitchen and dropped his briefcase. That sound—he'd never heard anything like it. It was part scream, part agony. It echoed against his walls, infiltrating every inch of his home.

He ran for the stairs, taking them two at a time, bypassing Nate's still-quiet bedroom—thank God—and headed for Georgia's room at the far end of the long hall. There were no longer words. Just high-pitched, seemingly endless screams.

Questions ran through his head. Had someone broken in? He slowed, steps from Georgia's door. Should he retrieve his gun from the safe?

The screaming grew louder, and Eric picked up the pace. He didn't have time to get a weapon. He'd fight the intruder with his bare hands. He'd help her. Save her. There was no other option.

Eric pushed through the unlocked door, ready to fight. But the second he saw Georgia, his hands fell to his sides.

She lay on her bed, twisting and turning, her face damp from perspiration, her beautiful features contorted in agony and fear. She was alone, but that offered little comfort. Whatever was terrorizing her was on the inside.

Chapter Fifteen

"GEORGIA, WAKE UP!"

She heard the familiar voice. It cut through the
images, pushing aside the terror. She no longer felt Louis's body pinning her down, holding her in the open. The
sounds—the rapid gunfire, the yelling—faded. The cloud
of smoke she was fighting to breathe through vanished.

"Eric?"

"I'm here." His hands pressed into her shoulders,
drawing her up into a seated position. Her clothes clung
to her damp body as she blinked, slowly taking in her
surroundings. Her room at Eric's house. The overhead
light was on. He must have hit the switch. She glanced
down, focusing on her breathing, knowing she needed
the steady in and out to find her way back.

She dug her fingers into the sheets twisted around her.
No one was shooting at her. Not here. She wasn't carrying
her friend's body. She stared at her knuckles, watching

them turn white, clutching the thin fabric. Nothing would hurt her here.

Except for her memories.

But only if she let them.

"You had a nightmare."

Georgia looked up at Eric and saw the concern on his face. "Yes."

"Georgia, you're shaking." He moved to the bed, drawing her into his arms, engulfing her in his strong embrace.

"I know." She breathed—in and out, burying the nightmare, beating back the terror. But the fear was still very much alive for him, she realized. He held her tight, as if the physical contact could literally keep her together.

But she wasn't breaking. Not now, not ever.

"It was just a bad dream," she said, fighting the slight tremble in her voice.

"The way you screamed…" His tone was rough with emotion as he reached for her, touching the side of her face. "It was pure terror."

She captured his hand in hers, offering a reassuring squeeze. "I know."

"This has happened before?"

She nodded. "Not for a while. But yes, it has."

"Why didn't you tell me?"

"I was handling it."

"By not sleeping," he said grimly, as if he was starting to put the pieces together. "Georgia, that's not a solution. You need help."

"I told you, I've got this. I'm working through it."

Eric raised his hand to her face, holding it there before brushing her cheek. The way he touched her was as if she were a scared animal. "Georgia, let me help you. Please. I love you. And seeing you like this…Christ, it tears me apart."

She pushed free from his embrace and stood, willing her trembling limbs to hold her steady. *Love.* That one word gave her strength and cut her to the core at the same time. She wanted his love, but not like this, not tied so closely to pity and anxiety.

Eric rose too, reaching for her. She stepped back.

"Eric, look at me." His eyes, still deep pools of seemingly bottomless worry, met hers.

"Do not mistake this for weakness," she said. "I am strong. Don't you dare doubt that. Ever. I don't need you to be my hero. I don't need you to protect me from my own memories. I don't need a white knight rushing in to save me. I'm my own hero. And I will get through this."

"Georgia, it's OK to ask for help. That doesn't make you weak. You went to war—"

"Uncle Eric?" The sound of Nate's half-asleep little-boy voice filled the space. Eric crossed the room in two steps, crouching in front of his nephew.

"Hey there, buddy," he said, his voice gentle and soft.

"Is there a bear in Georgia's room?" Nate asked, rubbing his eyes.

"No, Nate," he said. "No bears."

She watched as he pulled Nate into his arms, hugging him tight, offering the comfort Georgia had refused.

"I had a nightmare," she said. "I'm sorry I woke you, kiddo. It won't happen again."

Eric drew back from his nephew and looked over his shoulder at her. She saw the uncertainty in his expression. Then Eric returned his gaze to the scared, still-half-asleep child. He was trying to choose, she realized.

"It's not a choice," she said. "I'm fine. Take Nate back to bed."

Eric nodded. He stood and walked over to her. "I'll be back once he's asleep." He kept his voice low to ensure his words were not overheard. "I promise. Wait here for me. We'll talk."

"Eric, I'm fine," she insisted, knowing deep down it was a lie. But this wasn't his battle to fight.

He rested his hand on her shoulder and gave her a squeeze. "I'm going to help you through this, Georgia."

"Go," she said firmly. "Nate needs you."

Georgia watched Eric lift Nate into his arms. The little boy looked so small compared with his uncle. But he was safe there, right where he belonged.

"Night, Georgia," Nate mumbled, resting his cheek against his uncle's shoulder. "Maybe we can have pancakes in the morning. With syrup."

"Maybe, kiddo," she said. "Maybe."

Georgia waited until the sound of Eric's footsteps on the wooden floorboards faded, then she sat on her bed, drawing her knees tight against her chest. She picked up the sheet and wrapped it around her shoulders, draping it over her legs. Now that she was alone, the tears threatened.

"I'm strong," she whispered. "I know I am."

She closed her eyes, letting the teardrops flow freely. The nightmare, the fear, was all in the past. But the way Eric had looked at her? As if she were weak? As if his love was wrapped in pity? That hurt nestled deep inside. But what scared her the most was the way he looked back at her after Nate came into the room, as if he had to choose, as if he couldn't be enough for both of them.

And that was just plain wrong. Eric had infused her life with stability. She knew he did the same for Nate. His willingness to listen had helped strengthen her, allowing her to crack open the locks holding back her emotions.

But maybe he was right. Maybe it all came down to a choice. Deep down, she knew she couldn't stay here. Not if her nightmares disturbed the small child living down the hall. Nate had to come first. Always. She could still care for the little boy, even if she lived at her brother's house for a while, until the nightmares went away for good. And they would. She'd make sure of it.

A new wave of tears threatened. But this time Georgia fought back, squeezing her eyes tight against them. She refused to wallow. Pushing off the bed, she stripped off her damp nightclothes and pulled on the jeans and T-shirt she'd been wearing earlier. Gathering the keys to her borrowed Jeep, she headed for the door. Right now, she needed to feel the wind in her hair. She needed to feel alive, strong, and in control—because she was all of those things.

ERIC SAT ON the floor beside Nate's toddler bed, running his hand through the little boy's hair. His nephew had closed his eyes the minute his head hit the pillow, but Eric had stayed, wanting to make sure Nate was settled before he went back down the hall to Georgia. Was this what his father felt, he wondered, torn between a child who'd needed him and a woman who owned his heart?

As a kid, Eric had hated his father for choosing the latter. The women. The first time, he'd understood. He'd loved his dad's girlfriend like a second mother. But then she'd left, breaking his heart. He'd been older than Nate at the time, but still too young to understand the fickle nature of relationships. They weren't permanent, not like a son's love for his parents. So why had his mother and father insisted on falling in love again and again?

Because walking away was impossible.

Eric looked down at Nate. He didn't want to drag his nephew down the same road he'd traveled as a child. But he refused to abandon Georgia when she needed him most.

Eric shook his head. He'd find a solution in the morning. Whatever it took to make things right for her and for Nate. Right now he needed to check on her. Eric shifted away from Nate's bed, slowly rising to his feet. He stepped forward and the floorboards creaked.

Nate's hand shot out, reaching blindly in space, his eyes still shut. "Stay."

"I will, buddy. I'm not going anywhere," he said, grabbing hold of his nephew's hand. Eric sank to his knees beside the bed. He found one of Nate's stuffed animals, placing it under his head as he stretched out on the floor. Another few minutes and the kid would be sound asleep. Then he could go to Georgia.

Staring up at the ceiling, Eric heard footsteps in the hall. Panic rose, his stomach somersaulting as his blood seemingly ran cold.

Georgia was leaving.

Eric closed his eyes. His world rushed headlong into a downward spiral, shifting beyond his control. Here, in this little boy's room, a stuffed animal under his head for a pillow, he felt as if he'd been thrust back in time. He'd been on the verge of falling for her. He'd wanted to believe they could have a future together. And she was walking away.

No. He couldn't let her go. He refused to lose her.

Eric sat up and reached for Nate's stuffed froggie. Slowly, he pulled his hand free from Nate's smaller one, offering the frog in its place. Lost in sleep, the little boy snuggled up to the stuffed animal.

"I'll be right back, buddy," he whispered.

Nate didn't move. Eric silently rose to his feet, tiptoed out of the room, and burst into a run when he hit the hall. He took the stairs two at a time.

"Georgia!" He raced into the kitchen. He caught a glimpse of her brown hair. The door leading to the garage closed behind her. He followed, catching up with her as she opened the door to the Jeep. She froze, one hand in the open driver's side window. He saw her red eyes and knew she'd been crying. But the way she held herself, her shoulders back, her head high with her hair flowing freely over her shoulders, she looked beautiful, strong, so damn determined.

"Don't leave," he said. "Stay and talk to me. Please, Georgia."

Lips pursed, she shook her head. "I need to do this on my own."

"No, you don't." He stepped down into the garage, moving closer, needing to pull her into his arms. She belonged here, with him.

"I do." She climbed into the car, closing the door, shutting him out.

"If you want to do the right thing for me and for Nate," she said through the open window, "let me go. I can't...I can't do this. Us. I thought I could, but...I'm sorry."

He saw the chink in her armor when she said the word *us*, as if being with him was her Achilles' heel, the one thing that could tear her apart when what she needed right now was to come back into her own.

Georgia turned the key and pressed the button to open the garage door. Eric stepped back, releasing his hold on the car. Inside, his heart felt as if she'd taken an axe to it, splitting it open like a log. But if this was best for her and for the child upstairs...

Eric closed his eyes, his hands forming fists at his sides. He'd take a fucking chainsaw to his heart—anything—if it meant taking care of Georgia.

Chapter Sixteen

GEORGIA TURNED ONTO the two-lane, paved road and accelerated. Windows open, wind blowing, she watched the speedometer as it moved past the speed limit. Ten miles over. Twenty. Twenty-five over. Her pulse raced. She felt out of control, yet completely in charge at the same time. It was a heady rush.

"Just a little faster," she murmured, pressing her foot down. She craved more. The speed. The excitement pulsing through her.

Out of the corner of her eye, she spotted movement on the side of the road. Georgia slammed on the brakes. A deer leapt into the center of her lane and froze. Georgia silently prayed the car would stop in time, knowing if she jerked the wheel in one direction, she risked skidding into the ditch, or worse.

"Stop, stop, stop," she begged the car. If she hit that animal, if she killed it...No, she couldn't bear it. One more life wiped away, and this one all her fault.

Screeching, the Jeep stopped a few feet in front of the terrified animal. It blinked, staring at Georgia for a second before prancing to safety. A second, smaller deer followed.

"Oh, God," she whispered. "What have I done?"

Georgia slowly steered the car to the side of the road, out of the way of oncoming traffic. Leaning back in her seat, she closed her eyes. She'd been so desperate to escape her own feelings that she'd nearly killed an innocent animal.

Cars passed her on the left, and she knew it was only a matter of time before someone stopped to check on her. She couldn't stay here, but she was not ready to go back to Eric's house. She needed time and space to think. She had to find her way through this mess.

Georgia steered the Jeep back onto the road and headed for the one place she could always call home—her brother's house. Truth descended on her, and this time she couldn't escape it. She didn't want to run, not anymore. Hiding from the things that scared her most was no longer an option. The only thing that would make her feel alive was living her life to the fullest. No more wild adventures. If she wanted to live, she had to go after the things that mattered in her life.

Eric.

In the morning, she would return to Eric's home and fight for her future. She would find a way to explain that she needed him, not to solve her problems, but to love her.

Georgia parked the Jeep in front of Liam's modest ranch home, surprised to find the lights on. She had a key and had planned to slip in and retreat to the spare bedroom, the one she'd claimed when she first returned home from Afghanistan. She hadn't expected Liam to be awake.

Georgia slid out of the driver's seat and headed for the front door. It was open when she arrived, and her brother stood in the doorway, wearing a pair of ripped jeans and an old T-shirt inside out.

"I'm sorry. I shouldn't have come here. It's late." She glanced over her shoulder at the parking area for a second car.

"You're welcome here anytime," Liam said. "You know that, Georgie."

"Thanks, but if you have company, I can leave." She took a step back.

"I'm alone. Just couldn't sleep." He stepped back, holding the door open for her. "Come on in. Join me for a drink."

Georgia obeyed, heading for the kitchen.

"Since you're here, I'm guessing Eric told you," he said tightly, pulling two beers from the fridge.

"Told me what?"

Liam let out a mirthless laugh, and Georgia glanced around the kitchen, noting the empty beer bottles by the sink. Her brother didn't drink much. Rarely more than one or two beers, especially during fire season when the crews had to harvest trees whenever they could. More than two and he didn't feel comfortable operating the machinery the next day.

"Are you drunk?"

"Getting there. I bet Eric sent you here to check on me. You two are close. More so now that you're living with him. Are you sure he didn't ask you to come by and question me?"

"In the middle of the night? Why would I question you in the middle of the night?"

Liam set his mostly full beer on the counter. "The DOF is accusing me of running the equipment after one in the afternoon the day the fire started."

"What? But you didn't, right?"

"Hell, no. But Eric," Liam said, running both hands through his hair, "I'm not sure he believes me. Even if he does, if the DOF investigation concludes that I ordered the crew to run over, if they believe this goddamn anonymous tip, he won't have much choice. He'll have to fire me."

"Eric wouldn't do that."

Why hadn't Eric told her? She thought back to the other night, when he'd come home in a foul mood. He hadn't said a word.

Because when he'd mentioned real consequences—and nothing was more real than firing his best friend—she'd turned the conversation 180 degrees and focused it on her time in Afghanistan.

"He wouldn't fire you if you didn't do it," she said firmly. "Talk to him. He'll tell you the same thing."

"I don't think he'd have much choice," Liam said. "And shit, I told him not to tell you. He promised he wouldn't."

"He didn't say a word about the DOF and their accusations."

"Then why are you here? Did something happen?" Concern trumped his drunken state, and she could see Liam was ready to take on whatever had sent her running home.

"I had a nightmare." She proceeded to tell him about waking up and needing to go for a drive, leaving out the part when Eric burst in to save her or Nate woke up afraid that bears had invaded her room. She explained about the deer in the road.

"I realized how foolish I've been, trying to feel alive instead of focusing on living, instead of opening up to the people around me."

"You weren't foolish," he said, crossing the room and pulling her into a hug. "You did some stupid things, but maybe that's what you needed. Don't give yourself too much grief. That's what I'm here for." He drew back and smiled down at her. "So this focus on living? What does that mean?"

"Not driving too fast," she said. But she couldn't tell him the rest, not tonight. She wanted to wake up every day in love and surrounded by people she called family. It wasn't a cure-all. She'd still have nightmares, possibly other setbacks. But she wasn't going to let those hold her back. Not anymore.

"I guess that's a start," Liam said.

Georgia nodded. "I'll let you know when I figure out the rest."

"OK," he said. "Planning to crash here tonight?"

"Yeah, if you don't mind. I might need to stay for a while."

His smile faded. "Because of the nightmares? Or did things go south between you and Eric?"

"After the nightmare, I think it might be best. For Nate," she said. Right now, she couldn't say one way or the other where things stood between her and Eric. She only knew what she wanted from him. "We can figure it out later. Right now, I'd like to watch a movie on your couch. Maybe fall asleep."

"I'll join you," he said, stepping back, releasing his hold on her as he headed for the other room. "And if you fall asleep, don't worry. I'll stay up. You know, just in case you start to have a bad dream."

"Thank you." Georgia slid off her stool and followed him into the living room.

"I'm your big brother, Georgie. That's what I'm here for." He sat on the couch and picked up the remote. "But no chick flicks. I can't stay awake watching some shirtless dude."

She laughed, despite the swirling emotions inside. Liam was here for her, always. And how was she repaying him? Sleeping with his best friend and boss. But no, it wasn't just sex—she was falling in love with Eric. And she refused to walk away from love just because it was complicated.

Chapter Seventeen

ERIC WOKE TO small hands pushing against his shoulder. He opened his eyes. A stuffed giraffe stared back at him.

"Georgia says you have to get up."

Rolling until his back lay flat against the hardwood floor, Eric found Nate staring down at him. "She's here?"

Nate nodded, pointing to the door. Lifting his head, Eric spotted her, leaning against the entrance, holding a steaming cup. It was as if he was waking from his own nightmare. Except this time, Georgia had come back, leaving him wondering if he'd emerged in a dream.

"We let you sleep in as long as we could." She stepped into the room and held out the mug. "Coffee?"

"Thanks." He stood, tucking his dress shirt back into his pants before accepting her offering. After she'd driven away, he'd returned to Nate's side and spent the night in yesterday's suit. But that was only one reason he felt as if the lines between dream and reality had blurred. He'd watched her drive away last night and assumed he'd lost her. And now she was standing in front of him with a cup of coffee.

Lifting the mug to his lips, he studied her. She'd traded her jeans and T-shirt for a red polka-dot sundress with buttons running down the front and sandals. But the young, feminine clothes bore a sharp contrast to the determination he saw in her brown eyes.

"You came back," he said softly, unable to hide his awe. "I thought you were gone."

"I needed to think," she said. "And after I take Nate to school, we should talk."

"Whatever you need," he said. The idea of redefining this relationship, thrusting it back over the line, ripped at the raw, hurting place inside him. But he'd stand by those words and do as she asked. If it was in his power to help her, he would, no matter what it cost him.

AN HOUR LATER, Eric was sitting at the kitchen table, checking his email and notifying his assistant that he'd be arriving late this morning. He'd showered, shaved, and dressed for the day in a fresh suit, shoving his emotions aside as he went through the routine actions.

He'd called a few independent investigators, asking them to drop by his offices that afternoon. If the DOF insisted on blaming his crew, and Liam in particular, he wanted confirmation from an outside source before he let his best friend go.

"Is now a good time?"

He looked up. Georgia stood in the doorway, twirling her keys in her hand.

"Yes." He closed the laptop and stood, heading toward her. "Did Nate get to school OK?"

She nodded but didn't move from the doorway. "Were you planning to tell me about the fire investigation and Liam?"

Eric froze in the middle of his kitchen. "No. He asked me not to say anything. Not until we knew more. He didn't want to worry you. Who told you?"

"Liam did." She slipped the keys into a pocket hidden in her sundress and folded her arms across her chest. "I drove to his place last night. He thought you'd sent me to question him."

His hands formed tight fists. "Did you tell him the truth?"

She cocked her head, studying him. "I explained about my nightmare, but I left you out of it. And I didn't tell him about us. I couldn't. Not when he told me you might fire him."

"I'm hoping it won't come to that."

"Do you believe him? Do you think he is telling the truth about stopping the chainsaws before the fire restriction took effect?"

"I believe in his intentions," Eric said slowly. "I know he meant to do the right thing and follow the law. But there is a chance he tried to push the crew, to fell one last tree, and got too close to the time limit."

"No," she said firmly. "He didn't."

"I hope you're right." He wanted to believe his best friend. But he couldn't fudge the truth to protect him. Not when it came to a forest fire that had the potential to cost hundreds of people their lives, never mind the crews who'd worked around the clock to put out the blaze. It was one thing to overlook a spark. People made mistakes. It was another to violate the fire code. Even by a few minutes.

"Either way I'm hiring a private investigator to find out," he said.

"And until you learn the truth, you don't want to tell him about us."

He looked into her brown eyes, so familiar, yet different. "Georgia, last night, you said yourself that this— us—it's too much. And I think you're right. I think you need more time to heal. I want to do what is best for you."

He stepped closer, needing to touch her. But she moved to the side, out of his reach. "I'll be there for you, as a friend," he added. "Whatever you need. You have my word."

"You'll always be my friend, Eric," she said. "But I want more. After I left here last night…"

He saw the far-off look in her eyes and his concern snowballed. What had she done after she'd run from him last night? The idea of her seeking another rush flat-out terrified him. More than anything he needed her safe.

"After I left, I realized that the nightmares, the fears, those might always be a part of me. Hopefully, they'll fade. I don't know. I'll ask the shrink the next time I see him."

He raised an eyebrow. "You're going back to therapy?"

She nodded. "I have something to say. I'm ready to talk to him. And you know why? Because I've figured out how to live my life to the fullest."

"How?"

"I've fallen in love with you. You've always been a good friend, Eric. But what we have, it is more than sex. I trust you. I feel safe with you. But most important, I'm happy when I'm with you. You're my friend, I've loved you practically forever, and now I'm in love with you. What could be better than that?"

She'd fallen in love. Hope surged, but doubt rose quickly to greet it. "Georgia, after everything you've been through, after what you said last night, how can you be sure—"

"That I'm in love? I know what I feel, Eric. The guilt that I lived, the need to feel worthy, that is still there. It might never go away. Falling in love with you didn't 'fix' me. I was never broken.

"The other night you told me that who I am is enough. And you were right. I deserve to move forward with my life. I want to live every day to the fullest loving you. I want to spend the nights making love to you—wild, crazy, kinky, whatever you want, Mr. Straightlaced. I want to build a future with you. And you don't need to worry I'm going to bolt. I won't. I told you last night I'm strong. I can do this. Please say yes, Eric. Tell me you meant what you said last night when you told me you loved me."

"Georgia, it's not that simple." She'd spun a complete one-eighty in a matter of hours. He wanted to believe her words. But the idea of pushing her too far, of sending her running away again…

"Eric," she demanded, "did you mean what you said last night?"

"Georgia, I've always loved you," he said. "And now…"

"We're more. We're lovers," she said softly. "Don't be afraid, Eric. Not of this. Not of us."

"That's not it." Wasn't he supposed to be the one looking out for her fears? He didn't want to walk away. But he had to. For her.

"Eric, watch my hands."

He stepped back. "No, Georgia. We can't."

Georgia touched the top button on her dress, pushing it through the hole. Her hand dropped to the next one. He knew he should leave, but his feet remained rooted to the floor, unwilling to walk away from the woman who, right or wrong, had become necessary to his life.

She undid the next button and the one below that until the dress fell open, revealing the soft slopes of her breasts. Lifting her hands to her shoulders, she drew the fabric down her arms, slipping one arm out, followed by the next. She slid the dress down her body, releasing the fabric at her hips, allowing it to fall to the floor. Stepping out of the center, she reached behind her back and undid her bra. It fell away from her breasts, joining her dress on the floor. Her hands moved to her hips, stripping away her underwear as she closed the space between them.

"Georgia," he said, his voice strained.

She wrapped her arms around his neck. Staring up into his eyes, she ran her fingers through his short hair.

She'd always been beautiful. But there was something about the certainty of her movements and the way she touched him without hesitation. Georgia wasn't holding back. She was offering him everything—her body, her touch, her love.

But he couldn't take it.

"Georgia, we can't do this," he said, closing his eyes, resting his forehead against hers.

"Shh." She placed one finger over his lips. "Let me love you, Eric. Here. Now. It's just us. Marie's off today. Nate's at school. It's just you and me."

She arched up, capturing his mouth, kissing him deeply as he fought to hold back. But with every naked inch of her pressed against him, his willpower headed for the door. He'd figure this out. He swore he would. If he'd screwed up, he'd make amends and make damn certain he chose the right path forward.

He reached for her, running his hands up from her lower back. His mouth still locked on hers, taking everything she offered, he trailed his fingertips over her ribcage around to her chest.

Using his body, he guided her back to the wall beside the archway leading to the front room. He held her there. Kissing. Exploring. His palms brushed over her breasts, teasing and taunting.

Eric broke their kiss. Glancing down, he watched his rough hands move over her soft skin. She pressed her hands against the wall as if seeking support, and he moved his thigh between her legs. Georgia rubbed up against him, riding him, and hell, he wished he'd stripped out of his clothes.

"We'll make this right, I promise." His voice was a low growl and she moaned at the sound, arching into his touch. He traced small circles around her breasts.

"Georgia," he murmured, lowering his mouth to her neck. He pinched her nipples between his thumb and forefinger. She cried out, grinding her hips against his thigh. He could feel her growing wet through the fabric of his pants. He wanted to make her come just like this.

"Eric," she panted. "Eric, I—"

"Get your fucking hands off her!" The command came from the front door, punctuated by a slam.

Liam.

Every muscle in Eric's body tensed. He heard footsteps rushing from the front door toward the archway leading to the kitchen and debated stepping away from Georgia. But Eric didn't want her brother's first punch to hit her. Liam would never do it on purpose. Still, fury could push a person past control. Eric stayed, his clothed body shielding Georgia's naked one. If he moved, she'd be exposed.

Liam grabbed Eric's arm and pulled him off Georgia, his anger adding to his strength.

"What the hell were you thinking?" Liam demanded. "She's my sister!"

"Liam, please don't do this," Georgia said.

Liam ignored her, delivering a right hook to Eric's face. His head swung back, and he felt blood pool in his mouth. Eric stumbled back a step and then steadied himself, preparing for the next hit, knowing he deserved every one.

Chapter Eighteen

GEORGIA SCRAMBLED TO find her dress. She had to stop her brother. Eric refused to fight back, taking each hit as if he'd earned a penalty for loving her.

"Stop, Liam." She slipped her dress over her head, quickly buttoning up the front just enough to cover her chest. "This is not what it looks like."

She raced forward and grabbed her brother's arm. Liam stilled, unwilling to risk pushing her aside in order to hit his friend, the man she loved.

"It's exactly what it looks like," he said. "I trusted him and look what he fucking did."

"He didn't *do* anything," she said.

Liam turned to her. "You were naked, Georgia. In the damn kitchen. He had his hands all over for you. When I asked him to give you a job, I expected my best friend to keep you safe. Look after you. Not seduce you." Her brother's eyes narrowed. "Is this why you wanted to leave last night? Did he force you?"

"What?" Her eyes widened. "No! It's not like that. It's never been like that."

"Never?" Liam turned to Eric, baring his teeth like an angry animal intent on tearing something to shreds. "How long has this been going on?"

"A couple of weeks," Georgia said. "Not that it is any of your business. And we were planning to tell you after the investigation."

Her brother didn't look at her, instead focusing on Eric. "You've been sleeping with my sister for weeks and you didn't think to tell me because of some problem at work? What the hell? You're my fucking best friend. I respected you, Eric. How could you lay a hand on her knowing what she has been through? She's been back three months! Before that she was living in a war zone. And this is your way of helping her? I thought I could trust you to take care of her. But stripping her down and screwing her against the wall in broad daylight before she goes to pick up your kid? That's how you repay decades of friendship and trust?"

Georgia stepped between them. She'd had enough of the anger and accusations from her brother. And Eric still hadn't said a word. His face was a bloody mess and his eyes were downcast, as if he believed Liam's words.

"Eric didn't strip me down. I took off my own clothes, thank you very much," she said, meeting her brother's fury head-on.

"Georgia—"

"No. It's your turn to listen. He did nothing wrong. We fell in love." She pressed her index finger against her brother's chest. "And don't you dare tell me I can't handle that. I know what I'm capable of."

"No, Georgia, you don't," Liam snapped. "You had a nightmare just last night." Her brother looked over her shoulder at Eric. "Did she tell you about how she wakes up terrified? How she is afraid to sleep?"

"He knows, Liam. He's the one who woke me up."

Liam stepped around her, grabbing the front of Eric's shirt. "You know and you still thought, 'What the hell, I'll fuck her'?"

"Because he loves me and trusts me," she said. "Right, Eric?"

She moved to her brother's side, placing her hand over his. Liam released his hold on Eric's shirt. Georgia laid her palm over the place where her brother's had been—over Eric's heart.

"You love me," she said.

"I do, Georgia," Eric said finally. "You're my friend—"

"Not anymore, she's not," Liam growled. "If she were your *friend*, you'd have treated her with some goddamn respect."

Eric stood tall and strong despite his physical pain, but looking into his eyes, she could see his uncertainty. It was as if Eric believed her brother, as if he thought she didn't know her own heart.

"Enough, Liam," she said. Inside, her emotions ran wild. In a matter of minutes, feelings would overwhelm her, reduce her to tears and force her to acknowledge the simple fact that her heart was breaking. She was losing someone she loved, even though he was standing right there in front of her.

He'd been trying to explain, she realized. Earlier, when he'd held back, telling her he couldn't touch her, he was pushing her away. His reasons, whatever he used to justify walking away from love, didn't matter. Her list was longer, but she'd still come back and fought for him.

One tear escaped and she backed away. She refused to fall apart in front of Liam and Eric.

"I thought you were stronger." She looked at Eric. Blood dripped out of the corner of his mouth. She'd so rarely seen him out of control, except maybe for a moment that first night in his bedroom. But right now, he looked lost. "I thought you had the courage to follow your heart."

"Georgia—"

"Are you *in love* with me, Eric?" she pressed. "Because if you're not, nothing else matters."

"It's not that easy," he said.

Georgia bit her lip. Hard. Needing to feel something other than the rushing, all-consuming heartbreak.

"There are some things worth fighting for," she said. "Against all odds, in spite of the obstacles. I thought we were one of them. But I can't change how you feel. I can't make you fall in love with me."

She waited for him to object and admit that his love for her trumped everything.

"Georgia," he said. "I need to do what is best—"

"I'm leaving now." She turned away and went to retrieve her bag from the kitchen counter. She couldn't stand to hear him profess his desire to do the right thing again. "But I'll be back."

"You're not working for him and you're not living here," Liam ground out. "He can find a new nanny. You're moving home."

"No. I'm not staying here or moving in with you, Liam. I'll sleep at a friend's house. And I'll continue to care for Nate." She looked back at Eric one last time. "I'll never walk away from him. I love him too, and I refuse to let what happened between us hurt him. I'll be there when he gets out of preschool. Today and the day after that. You have my word."

Her head high, Georgia turned and headed for the door. She stepped into the garage and ran for the Jeep. Inside the car, she turned the key and backed out. She drove until she reached the main road. Once she felt certain they'd stayed behind to fight instead of chasing after her, she pulled out her cell and dialed.

"Hello?"

"Katie," she said, her voice wavering as the tears started falling. She couldn't hold them in any longer.

"What's wrong?" her friend said. "Did something happen? Are you OK?"

"Liam found out. And he threw punches," she said, fighting back a sob. "It's over. Between Eric and me. He's not in love with me."

"Oh, Georgia," she said. "I'm so sorry."

She drew a deep breath. "At least I wasn't afraid to go after him, right? I had the courage to fall in love. And he...well, he didn't."

"I don't think that's true," Katie said. "I believe Eric loves you."

"Not enough." Georgia closed her eyes. "Not enough."

Chapter Nineteen

GEORGIA WAS GONE. Eric stared out the kitchen window, watching the Jeep disappear down the drive. And this time, she wasn't coming back. Not for him.

"Forgetting for a minute that Georgia's my little sister," Liam growled, "I would have thought the idea of starting something with a woman who's likely to bolt would have kept you away. I was there every time one of your parents' new *friends* walked out, forgetting about you as quickly as they did your parents. Hell, by the time you were sixteen, you believed everyone who said they loved you would walk away. In all the years I've known you, you've never had a serious relationship. You were always waiting for the other shoe to drop."

Eric's hands balled into fists. The friend who knew him better than anyone else had just handed him the truth. So many people had vanished from his life, over and over again. Even his mother was leaving him behind soon.

Georgia's nightmares, his misplaced desire to do what he thought was right for her—those were excuses. That wasn't why he let her walk out of his life. He'd been so damn worried she couldn't be the person he required in his life that he hadn't stopped to ask if he could be the man she needed in hers.

And he wasn't. Not if he walked away at the slightest sign of trouble.

"Do you want Nate to grow up like that?" Liam pressed. "Do you want to watch your nephew's heart break when Georgia falls apart and runs away? Because it is only a matter of time, man. She's not the same person she was. We both know that. She's barely holding it together, moving from one rush to another. That's all you were, man, another high."

"Enough," Eric said firmly. "We were wrong to keep this from you. But don't you dare think less of Georgia. This wasn't about her finding another adrenaline hit."

"Yeah," Liam said with a grim laugh. "Keep telling yourself that."

"She went through hell, and she kept going. She's not weak, Liam."

"What about you?" Liam challenged. "Have you moved beyond your past? Because if you haven't, you had no right to touch Georgia."

"No, I haven't," he said, meeting Liam's intense stare. "And you're right, I should have stayed away. But I've cared for your sister for most of my life. I've wanted her for so long, and I knew what was at stake if I ever made a move."

Eric looked out the window at the pond. He could still picture Georgia poised to dive into the cold depths. "These past couple of weeks, I couldn't resist falling for her. I've never met a woman whose beauty ran so deep. Her courage, her sense of duty, her passion for living—Georgia is amazing inside and out. I love her. So much it scares me."

Liam folded his arms across his chest. "If you loved her so damn much, why'd you let her leave?"

"She is facing her demons head-on. But that doesn't mean they are gone. I was trying to do what is best for her. And for Nate."

And for himself. He'd been fighting hard to keep his heart safe. He'd thought if she could just commit to him. But she had, and he still couldn't believe she wouldn't walk away.

"But I fucked up," he said.

"Yeah, you did." Liam shook his head and opened the front door to the bright late summer day. "Not that it's worth much, but I still want your word you'll keep your hands off her."

Eric nodded. "You have it."

"Good." Liam gave a curt nod. "And I don't give a damn about the outcome of the investigation. You can consider this my resignation."

Eric watched his best friend walk out of his life, slamming the door behind him. Slowly, because every inch of his body was crying out in pain, he turned to the freezer. Opening the door, he pulled out a bag of peas and held it up to his jaw. He'd deserved every hit, but that didn't mean it hurt any less.

By the time you were sixteen, you believed everyone who said they loved you would walk away.

Eric closed his eyes. Liam's words felt like one of Georgia's arrows spiraling toward a target, hitting home and hurting more than the damage his best friend had done with his fists. And knowing he'd just let the woman he loved walk out of his life without a fight because he was afraid? That was the hit that drained the air from his lungs, leaving him leveled and heartbroken. Part of him wanted to go after her, but hell, after today?

"I don't deserve her."

Chapter Twenty

GEORGIA LAY ON Katie's bed, staring up at the pink horses dancing across the ceiling. She'd fought for what she wanted, faced her fears, and opened her heart. But it wasn't enough.

"Are you OK?" Katie stood in the doorway to her bedroom, dressed in her cowboy hat and jeans. Her friend had been out riding while Georgia lay here wallowing.

"You know, it's funny," Georgia said, sitting up on the four-poster bed fit for a nine-year-old little girl, not her twenty-something friend. "I feel more broken now than I did when I first returned home from Afghanistan. I just feel empty."

Katie came in, pulling the door closed behind her, and sat on the edge of the bed. "Have you talked to him?"

"Only a few words here and there when I arrive in the morning and again when he gets home at night. Nothing more than whether Nate ate breakfast or took a nap."

"You should," Katie said. "He's probably hurting too. And you should call your brother."

Georgia flopped back on the bed, returning her attention to the horse wallpaper. "Did Liam stop by again?"

"Yeah, but my brothers chased him away." Katie set her hat on the wooden dollhouse in the corner.

"That was nice of them."

Katie crawled up on the bed beside her. "Trust me, it was their pleasure."

"You know, I've never understood why they don't like Liam," Georgia said. "They've always been friendly with Eric."

"They had a fight," Katie said. "Years ago. My brothers are good at holding a grudge. It's a family trait. Even if they liked him, they'd keep him away for you. They don't know the details. And I don't plan to tell them. But they know you're hurting."

"Because I spend all my free time holed up in your room staring at your wallpaper?"

Katie laughed. "Yeah. That's part of it."

"I know I can't stay here forever. Tomorrow I'll start looking for an apartment." Georgia rolled to her side and propped up her head with her hand. "You could move in with me. Live in a room that isn't decorated for an elementary school student. And your three brothers wouldn't be down the hall."

"Tempting, but I need to live close to my horses. I don't plan to move until I have enough saved to take them with me. If that day ever comes, and that's a big *if* given my measly salary from the company, I'm going far away, not an apartment in town," Katie said. "And I'm still hoping you'll work things out with Eric."

Georgia sighed. "I think you're the only one."

"I wouldn't be so sure of that," Katie said. "You should have a little faith in him. He lost his best friend and the woman he loves in a single morning. Give him a few days to get his act together."

"He's not in love with me." If he was, he'd fight for her, wouldn't he? Love and life—those were worth fighting for, no matter what the circumstances. They were so lucky to have the opportunity to fall in love, to have found each other. Why couldn't he see that?

"He's just scared. We all are sometimes," Katie said.

Georgia stared at a purple horse. "If he's scared," she said slowly, "it's not for himself. He's afraid for Nate's sake. He would give up everything to do what he believes is right for that little boy."

"He's wrong," Kate said quickly.

"I know. But if I were in his shoes, faced with a person struggling with nightmares and memories that scare me to my core, I'd probably do the same thing. I know I'm strong enough to move past it all. But for him? It's a gamble. One he's not in a position to make without risking Nate."

Georgia closed her eyes. "That makes me love him even more. I told Eric the other night that I don't need a hero. And I don't. But that little boy does. He needs Eric to be his hero and stand up for what he believes is in the kid's best interest."

Katie took hold of her hand and squeezed it. "Pushing you away? That's not what's right for Nate. One day he is going to figure that out."

"Maybe." Georgia wasn't so sure. Eric's moral compass saw the world in black and white. And believing in her—that choice was squarely in the gray column.

ERIC SAT AT the kitchen table staring at the private investigator's findings. Neither the DOF or the team he'd hired had determined the fire's point of origin, but his guy had uncovered something that changed the entire investigation. Forty-eight hours had passed since his fight with Liam, but Eric couldn't keep this information from him. It didn't matter that it was late, practically the middle of the night. He had to call.

He punched the numbers into his cell. It rang and then went to voice mail.

"Hey, it's Eric. I thought you might like to know that the private investigator discovered that the anonymous tip the DOF received? It was placed by B&B Trucking. The day we fired them. I'm passing this information along to Caroline Smith. Should put you in the clear. And for what it is worth, I'm sorry I doubted you."

Eric ended the call and set the phone down on the kitchen table. He had a feeling it was only a matter of time before Liam was cleared of any wrongdoing. Determining where the fire started would help. He hoped that Caroline would have that key piece of the puzzle by tomorrow's meeting. But knowing how something started didn't change the outcome. Liam could have played by the rules and still missed a smoldering spark let off by a chainsaw. Sometimes it came down to human error.

Eric knew what had pushed him from friends to lovers with Georgia. One dropped towel on his bedroom floor combined with years of love and longing. Knowing that didn't change the fact he had no idea what to do next. The uncertainty, not knowing which was the correct path, ate at him day and night.

"Uncle Eric?" Nate appeared in the doorway, wearing his train pajamas and dragging his froggie.

Eric pushed back from the table and crossed to his nephew, crouching in front of him. "What's up, buddy? I thought you were asleep."

"I woke up." He rubbed his eyes with his free hand. "I need to make a sign."

"Can it wait until the morning?"

"No." The way he said that one word left little room for argument. "I need to do it now. Can you get my markers?"

"Sure." Eric scooped him up and headed for Nate's room. If he refused, Eric knew he'd be walking straight into tantrum territory. Right now, he didn't have the energy.

Eric set his nephew down. He retrieved the markers and a piece of construction paper, setting them on the child-size table. "What's the sign for?"

"To tell the bears to go away," Nate said, sliding into a seat at the table.

Eric glanced around the room. "There are bears in here again?"

"Not my room." Nate opened the green marker and drew a big X and a circle. "Georgia's. If I put a sign on her door, the bears will stay away. And then Georgia can come home."

Eric studied his nephew as he drew a second X on the page. How could he tell a little boy that he couldn't fight these bears because they haunted someplace within Georgia's mind? He pulled the second little chair beside Nate's and sat.

"That's a good idea, buddy," he said. "I'm sure Georgia will appreciate the sign. But I don't know if she can move back here. She'll still be here for you during the days."

He was so damn grateful Georgia had stayed true to her word, continuing in her role as Nate's nanny after things fell apart between them. But every day when she showed up, full of smiles for his nephew, it became more and more evident that he'd been the one holding back. Georgia would never walk out of Nate's life, subjecting him to the roller coaster Eric had ridden as a child.

Nate looked up from his paper. "I need tape."

"OK." Eric stood and went to the craft bin. He tore off a piece of Scotch tape. "Here you go."

Tape on his finger and the sign in his other hand, Nate headed for the door. Eric followed him down the long hall to Georgia's former room. Carefully, Nate placed the tape on the top of the paper and secured it to her door.

"Now she can come back," Nate said, looking up at him. "She needed help fighting the bears. Just like you help me when I'm scared. I helped Georgia."

"Yeah you did, buddy." Eric patted his shoulder, wondering how a toddler could be so damn wise. "But now it's back to bed."

They walked back to Nate's room and Eric tucked him in, kneeling beside his bed while Nate drifted off to sleep.

Eric knew he'd made the wrong call when he'd let Georgia go instead of helping her fight her bears. But he'd always thought it would be easy. He'd thought that when a child's heart was at stake, as his had been so many times growing up, there would be a definitive line between right and wrong. He'd been so determined to take the correct road, even if it tore him to pieces, that he'd put on blinders. There was one big difference between his parents' relationships and his own.

Georgia.

He'd fallen in love with a woman who was steadfast and sure, especially when it mattered. She'd never walk away from the people she loved. She had a razor-sharp view of what was important in life born from witnessing firsthand how fast it could all slip away. He'd viewed her experiences and memories as a handicap. Eric had willingly followed her brother down that path. But they were her greatest strength. Georgia refused to give up. She didn't walk away from love because it was difficult or complicated. She fought to find a way through.

"I don't deserve her. Not after the way I let her go," he whispered to the sleeping child. "But starting tomorrow, I'll do whatever it takes to win her back and prove that I love and need her. That we need her. I promise. I won't let her fight the bears on her own."

Chapter Twenty-One

ERIC WALKED INTO the Department of Forestry conference room wishing he could fast-forward through the next thirty minutes. He'd planned to be at home when Georgia brought Nate back from preschool. But then Caroline had moved the time of this supposedly informal meeting. The best he could hope for now was to get there by nap time. He was ready to beg. Whatever it took to win her back. He would have confronted her this morning while Nate was in school, but Caroline Smith had originally set this get-together for nine-thirty.

Settling into a chair at one end of the rectangular table, close to the door, Eric glanced at his watch. Georgia should be picking Nate up right now.

A hand touched his shoulder and Eric looked up. Caroline Smith, dressed in a fitted black pantsuit that accentuated her curves, smiled down at him. "Good morning. Glad to see you're healing. I heard about your fight with Liam Trulane."

"A scuffle among friends," he said. He'd refused to offer any insights into what had caused the fight. Most people, including Caroline, probably believed it had everything to do with the investigation. Eric had neither confirmed nor denied anything, unwilling to let the rumors touch Georgia.

"You'll be pleased to know we traced the fire back to its point of origin," Caroline added.

"Good." It had taken them long enough. But he couldn't tell from her expression if it was good news for Moore Timber, or if it further implicated Liam and his crew. "Where'd it start?"

"Why don't we wait for everyone else?" she said.

Two men Eric didn't recognize walked into the room carrying file folders overflowing with paper. Lawyers? Eric frowned. He'd brought legal representation to the first meeting, but after the investigation and questions dragged on and on, he'd decided to curtail the number of billable hours he was investing. Even if the DOF determined they'd made every reasonable effort to prevent the fire, he would be on the hook for a large portion of the expenses associated with fighting the flames. Why pay a lawyer to sit and listen to Caroline too?

More people came in, some of whom Eric knew from the DOF office. The private investigator he'd hired slipped into the room, claiming a chair around the wall. Eric drummed his fingers on the table, stealing a second glance at his watch. Georgia should be arriving home right about now.

"Welcome." Caroline Smith stood at the head of the table. "Thank you for coming today. Before we get started, I wanted to thank Moore Timber for their cooperation. Eric, you've been a real asset to this investigation."

Eric nodded. "Of course."

"The law presumes that if a fire occurs during an operation, it is the result of that operation," Caroline said.

What the hell? Every person in this room knew the DOF rules and regulations. Couldn't she get to the point?

"We initially suspected that the White Rock fire started where Moore Timber was harvesting," Caroline continued.

In his pocket, his cell vibrated. Eric pulled out his phone and checked the screen. Nate's preschool. He frowned and stood. "Please excuse me. I need to take this."

He didn't look back as he pushed through the door and quickly redialed the school. "This is Eric Moore. I missed a call."

"Mr. Moore," a warm voice replied. "This is Ms. Marianne, Nathaniel's teacher. Your nephew is here—"

"Is everything OK?"

"Oh yes," Ms. Marianne assured him. "He's fine. But his nanny did not come to pick him up. It is our policy to call after thirty minutes, but Nate was getting a little anxious."

"Georgia didn't show up?" Dread wrapped around him, clouding him in questions. Was she in trouble? Or had she run away? Georgia had promised she'd never walk away from Nate. But what if, just this once, she hadn't been strong enough? What if the stress she lived with day in and day out had won?

"Not yet, Mr. Moore. It's possible she is on her way, but we tried the number we have on record for her and no one answered." The teacher dropped her voice. "Nate's worried that bears might have attacked her. He was starting to get worked up, so I told him I'd call you."

Bears. Eric was wondering that same thing. Only he knew that Georgia's worst enemy did not have fur and claws. And if Georgia's memories made her run, there was no hope for their future.

"I'll be right there," Eric said. He ended the call and opened the door to the conference room. Caroline was still at the podium. He tuned her out, quickly gathering his briefcase, shoving his legal pad inside.

"I need to leave. Family emergency," he said. "I look forward to reviewing your findings." He pushed through the door, ignoring the exclamations from the filled conference room, and headed for his car.

Fifteen minutes later, he was inching down the two-lane road leading from the center of town to Nate's pre-school. Somewhere up ahead was an accident. Eric pulled out his cell and scanned his contacts. He'd tried Georgia twice. No answer. He'd even called Liam, but had been sent straight to voice mail again. There were only a handful of people whom he trusted to pick up Nate. He picked the one who lived on the other side of Nate's preschool, out in the farm country surrounding the town and away from this traffic nightmare.

"Katie," he said when Georgia's friend picked up. "I need your help." He explained about the call from school and his missing nanny.

"I'm happy to pick up Nate," she said. In the background, he heard Katie moving around, collecting her things. "But I don't understand. Georgia left here with plenty of time to run a few errands in town and get to Nate's school."

"If she stopped in town, she might be stuck in this traffic," he said, hoping that was the answer.

He ended the call with Katie and focused on the cars ahead of him. A pair of ambulances sped past him in the oncoming traffic lane, sirens blaring. Cop cars followed, then a fire truck.

Slowly, the cars in front of him inched forward. The cops had probably started directing traffic. Minutes later, he was at the scene, waiting his turn to bypass the first responders. He glanced left, scanning the area of the accident. He spotted two cars, a small four-door red one wrapped around a tree, and an upside-down Jeep.

His Jeep. The one he'd lent to Georgia.

Icy cold descended on him, numbing his body as his heart raced. It beat so fast, he felt as if it would explode in his chest. He swerved out of his lane and pulled over to the side of the road. A second later, he was out of his car and running. He had to get to her. Georgia. He couldn't lose her. Not now. Not like this. Not to a car accident.

A wreck had claimed his sister's life. But losing Georgia like this was another layer of hell. She was his heart. And he'd been too goddamn afraid to take the risk and fight for her.

Eric sprinted toward the Jeep. She'd offered love and strength to him and Nate. In a few short weeks, she'd become family. If by some miracle he was granted a second chance, he'd prove to her that he'd been wrong to let her go. So damn wrong.

A paramedic grabbed his arm. Eric tried to keep moving forward, nearly pulling them both to the ground.

"Hey, man, you can't go over there," the guy said.

"That's my car," he said. "Georgia's in there. She's my—" Nanny? Best friend's little sister? Friend? Lover? She was all those things and so much more.

"She's my everything," he said.

"OK, man." The paramedic wrapped his arm around Eric's back, holding him shoulder to shoulder. "We're going to get her out. Trust the guys to do their job."

"She's my everything," Eric repeated. "But I never told her."

Chapter Twenty-Two

GEORGIA OPENED HER eyes. She remembered the car and the white-haired, wide-eyed man behind the wheel. She'd seen a woman too, in the passenger seat. She was young and pretty, probably about Georgia's age. The white-haired driver had sped toward her, crossing the double line. He had been going so fast, too fast. She'd swerved, avoiding a head-on collision. And then she'd lost control. She remembered the Jeep turning over.

And fear. The memory of her panic was crystal clear. It had paralyzed her. She'd lived through months in Afghanistan to die here? In a car accident? No, that couldn't be right. Her mind rallied, fighting to stay present, to keep living. For Eric. For her brother. For herself. And for Nate.

Nate—she was supposed to pick him up. Now. Who would get Nate? That was her last clear memory before the pain won and she'd briefly drifted into nothing.

But now, she was awake. Alive. But still in the Jeep.

She blinked, slowly assessing her injuries. Her head throbbed, but the pain where the belt pressed against her lap was worse. Probably because she was hanging upside down and that belt was the only thing keeping her from landing on the car's ceiling. Or what was left of the crushed roof.

Broken glass—the windshield—covered everything she could see. She tried turning her head, angling for a closer look. Pain shot through her. She moaned, closing her eyes.

"Ma'am?" A man's voice called to her. "Can you hear me?"

"Yes." The word felt awkward on her tongue, and she tried again. "Yes, I can."

"We're going to get you out of there," he said. "The firefighters are working now."

"If I can reach the buckle," she said, lifting her hand. She could get herself out of here and find the voice. "I can crawl through the window."

"No, ma'am. Please try to remain still. We'll get you out," the voice said. "Until we determine the extent of your injuries, try not to move."

"I can do it," she said. She wasn't safe here, upside down. Hurting. Trapped. "I need to get out."

She reached again for the buckle. Pain shot through her arm. So intense. So strong. She tried to fight it. Her head swam. Darkness descended. She pushed against it. But her strength—it wasn't there.

"She's breathing." It was the same voice. "Checking for bleeding."

Hands moved over her limbs. She opened her eyes and saw nothing but blue sky, clear, no clouds. She tried to turn her head and realized she was strapped down. When they'd pulled her out, they must have strapped her to a backboard.

"Ma'am?" A young man hovered over her. "Can you tell me your name?"

"Georgia," she gasped, struggling to form the words. "Why are we out in the open?"

"We're moving you to an ambulance now." He looked up and a second later the stretcher beneath her shifted, rocking forward.

She studied the man. He wore a paramedic's uniform. But not military. She was home. She closed her eyes. A car accident. The white-haired man. She remembered. She hadn't been strong enough to get out, to stay awake.

"Do you know what day it is?" the paramedic asked.

Georgia searched her memory, but came up blank. She went back, starting at breakfast. She'd made eggs for Nate when she got to work, not pancakes.

"It's a school day," she said. "I need to pick Nate up from school."

"Your son?" he asked, his gaze sharp as he looked down at her.

She tried to shake her head, but couldn't. "No. I'm his nanny. But he's counting on me. I need to get to him. Please, you have to let me up."

"Not yet, Georgia. We need to get you to the hospital and assess your injuries," he said. "We'll call Nate's school and his parents."

She heard sirens blaring. They were close, but unable to turn her head, she couldn't see them.

"The other car," she said, panic rising again, unbidden and unwelcome. "What happened to the other car? The driver? Is he OK?"

"He's in critical condition," the medic said. "They're taking him to the hospital now."

"And the passenger?" The woman, young and pretty...

The paramedic hesitated, glancing at someone she couldn't see. "I don't know," he said.

But he did. Georgia knew he did.

"She died," Georgia said. The stranger, about her age, her whole life ahead of her—she was gone.

"Let's focus on you, Georgia."

The pain faded into the background, replaced by a storm of guilt. She'd lived. Her mind fragmented. It was too much, too overwhelming. For the first time since she'd returned home, she felt as if she were shattering.

Her breaths came in short, strangled gulps for air. The stretcher stopped.

"We're here." She heard the paramedic's voice. They'd reached the ambulance earmarked for her. She heard one of the men open the doors and hop inside.

The other turned to her. "Ma'am, are you OK? Deep breaths."

"I need to get to them." She fought for air, needing to speak. "The people in the other car. Please. I need them to live."

The medic bent over her, his brow furrowed with concern. But he shouldn't be worried about her. She'd lived. The others—he needed to help them.

Her strength? Where was it? Her hands balled into fists. Why would it fail her now? She closed her eyes. Pushing hard against the panic.

"I've got you." Fingers laced through hers, squeezing her hand tight. "Georgia, trust me. I've got you."

Georgia opened her eyes. "Eric."

"I'm here. I won't leave you. I'm not letting go." He leaned over, his face and those serious blue eyes blocking out everything else.

The terror receded, but she felt herself reaching for it, clinging to it. "Nate," she said. "I didn't get him."

His fingers brushed her cheek. "He's OK. Katie picked him up."

"The people," she said. "In the other car—"

"Don't worry about them. Not now, Georgia," he said. "I need you to stay with me. I was so damn afraid I'd lost you."

"The passenger died. She's dead," she said softly, staring up at Eric, begging him to understand. She couldn't do this again. She couldn't handle being the one who lived. It was too much.

He leaned down, his mouth close to her ear. "Close your eyes, Georgia. Picture the pond behind the house.

Imagine the water and the cold. You lived. Feel it. Let everything else go."

She obeyed, closing her eyes as they lifted her into the ambulance. Eric remained with her, holding her hand, never letting go.

"You don't have to be strong," he said. "Not this time. I'm here and I'm not going anywhere. I promise."

Chapter Twenty-Three

ERIC PACED BACK and forth in front of the local hospital, cell phone pressed to his ear. It rang and rang, then switched over to voice mail.

"Liam, pick up the damn phone," he growled. "Georgia was in a car accident. She's fine. Cuts, scrapes, a sprained wrist, and a concussion. They're keeping her for observation and to run a few more tests. According to the cop who stopped by, it looks like she was hit by a drunk driver."

Eric paused, staring up at the clear blue sky. Only a few hours had slipped by since he'd received the call from Nate's preschool, but it felt like years.

"I've got her, Liam," he said before the voice mail cut him off. "I love her and I'm not letting go. Not this time. Not ever again. But you should be here too. You're her family. So get your ass over here."

He ended the call and turned to go back inside. He wanted to talk to Georgia's doctors. He wasn't family. Not yet. But right now, he was the closest thing. And someone needed to look out for her.

"Uncle Eric!"

He turned and spotted his nephew running up the curved sidewalk, holding Katie's hand. Eric dropped to one knee, gathering the little boy in his arms. "Hey, buddy. I'm sorry I couldn't come get you today." He drew back, running his hand through Nate's hair. "Are you OK?"

"What happened to Georgia?" he demanded, his eyes wild with fear and worry.

Eric glanced up at Katie. He'd told her to keep Nate away from the scene of the accident, and then he'd sent a quick text asking her to meet him here. But he hadn't offered instruction on how to tell a three-year-old who'd lost his parents in a car crash he probably didn't remember about today's events. Hell, he didn't have a clue.

Katie shook her head, and he guessed she hadn't said much.

"Georgia was in a car accident," he said.

"She's in heaven now?"

"No," Eric said quickly. "She's fine. She hurt her arm and a couple of other places, but she is OK. You can see for yourself. When the doctors finish taking care of her, we'll visit."

Nate nodded, looking past Eric to the automatic double doors at the hospital's entrance. "They gave her a Band-Aid?"

Eric stood and took his nephew's hand. They headed for the doors with Katie following close behind. "Yeah, they gave her some Band-Aids."

"What kind? Superhero or train?"

"I don't know. We'll have to ask her," he said. "But my guess is superhero."

She'd been pulled from a totaled car, and still she'd been worried for the drunken fool in the other vehicle. She'd gone to war and returned stronger than the people she'd left behind. She'd opened her heart to him, a man who in many ways was still as caught up in childhood as the little boy she cared for, afraid everyone he loved would abandon him. And she'd stayed, when it would have been so much easier and safer to walk away. As far as he was concerned, that was the definition of superhero.

ERIC WALKED INTO her hospital room, and relief washed over her. He'd been her rock today, solid and stable when she'd crumbled. The wreck, knowing the passenger in the other car died, left her shaken. But he'd been there, holding her together. He'd asked for her trust, and she'd given it. It was as if she'd leapt off a cliff. Loving him was one thing. But believing he'd be there, ready and waiting to break her fall, to pick up the pieces? In that moment, when he'd held her hand, she'd understood for the first time that she didn't have to be strong every minute of every day.

Because she had him.

Her arm ached and her head felt as if she'd witnessed an IED blast, but still, it was as if a great weight had been lifted. The nightmares, the fears—she was going to put them behind her. One day. Not because she was strong or had frozen the memories in the pond. She'd move forward because love and trust were on her side.

"Georgia!"

She'd been so focused on the man she hadn't seen the little boy holding his hand. Nate ran to the side of her bed. Katie followed them into the room, a soft smile attempting to mask the concern in her friend's eyes.

"Hi, kiddo," Georgia said.

"Did you get a Band-Aid?" he demanded.

Georgia laughed, and even though her side ached and her muscles screamed for her to stop, it felt good. "More than one."

The sound of boots hitting the ground, like an elephant leading a race, echoed in the hall. Holding Nate's hand with her good one, she glanced at the door.

"Georgia." Liam rushed in, moving to the side of her bed. He lowered his forehead to hers and hugged her tight. "You scared me. When I heard Eric's message. Jesus." He squeezed tighter. "I thought I'd lost you."

"I'm OK. No major damage. Promise."

He stepped back and looked her over, assessing for himself. "You're sure?"

She nodded. "Yeah, I'm sure. They're releasing me tomorrow. Just one night for observation. That's all."

"Good. That's good," he said. "You'll come home?"

Georgia hesitated. She knew she'd held on to her anger long enough. Liam loved her and had been trying his best to take care of her. When he'd walked into the kitchen and found her naked with his friend, he'd been trying to protect her. She might not need him to fight her battles for her, but he was her brother. He'd always try.

"I—"

"She's coming home." Eric stepped forward, moving beside Nate on the other side of her bed. "With me."

Liam's eyes narrowed as he stared at Eric across her bed. But Eric ignored him, turning to her. He raised one hand, running his fingertips down her cheek.

"I was wrong, Georgia. I let you go. I told myself it was the best thing for you and for my family. I hid behind your traumatic experiences, when you were the one who faced your demons head-on. I let my childhood dictate my future when I should have fought for you."

He leaned down, brushing his lips over hers, a gentle kiss, but one given in front of her family and his. He pulled away and Georgia stared up at him, wondering if he understood how much she needed him in her life. How she'd realized that she was stronger with him, loving him, than apart.

"Eric," she whispered.

"I'm sorry, Georgia," he said. "Please come home. I'll be here for you every day. I'll help you heal, inside and out, no matter how long it takes. I swear I'll trust in your inner strength. If you promise you'll let me help you when you need it."

She nodded, feeling close to tears, but no longer caring who heard his magical words.

"Let me be your next big rush. Let becoming part of my family be your next big thrill," he said. "Georgia—"

"Yes," she said quickly. "Yes."

He raised an eyebrow but didn't say anything. She had a feeling she knew what he'd been about to say, and she didn't want to hear it. Not here. Not like this.

He'd told her he loved her before, while she was surfacing from a nightmare. Today, the wreck, and the dead woman from the other car—it felt like another terrible dream. When he said those words to her, she needed to know they came from the heart and were not wrapped up in fleeting panic and dread.

Fear touched every corner of her life. And that wasn't going to stop. Not today and probably not anytime in the future. But she didn't want it to be part of this moment with Eric.

THE NEXT MORNING, Eric and Nate picked her up at the hospital and brought her home. Eric took them out to lunch in town and, over burritos, asked about her doctor's follow-up instructions. The conversation moved from the side effects of a concussion to how many trains Nate could bring to show-and-tell at preschool.

No declarations of falling in love or promises of forever.

On the drive home, Georgia silently hoped the right moment would arise for Eric to declare his feelings. She wanted to hear those words. But Nate grabbed her hand the minute they walked in the door. He dragged her up the stairs and down the hall to the room she'd stayed in when she'd first become his nanny. Her hope hiccupped. When Eric had said those words back at the hospital—*becoming part of my family*—she'd envisioned different living arrangements.

"It's gone!" Nate cried.

Georgia crouched beside him. "What's missing, kiddo?"

"The sign!" he wailed.

She heard Eric's footsteps in the hall and turned. "Not gone. Just moved. Georgia will be sleeping in my room from now on."

The hiccups vanished as if she'd been holding her breath, waiting for confirmation. Eric scooped Nate up and took Georgia's good hand. He led them back down the stairs to his master bedroom. Now their room. Setting Nate on the floor, he pointed to the door. "There it is."

Georgia sank beside the little boy, studying the circles, dots, and Xs on the paper. "Did you make this, Nate?"

He nodded. "This sign will keep the bears away."

"Thanks, kiddo. It's perfect." Georgia drew him into a hug. Releasing the little boy just enough to see his face, she added, "You know what else helps keep the bears away?"

"What?"

"Waking up and remembering I have you and your uncle Eric."

She felt Eric's hand on her shoulder. He gave her a light squeeze.

"Always," he said. "Always."

Georgia spent the rest of the day playing trains, reading books, and watching Nate run in the yard. Eric fired up the grill and made steaks for dinner. Afterward, they put Nate to bed. Together.

Stepping out on the stone patio, monitor in hand, Georgia watched the sun sink behind the mountains.

"Thinking about a swim?" Eric came up behind her, wrapping his arms around her waist, drawing her back against him.

"The water's too cold this time of year," she teased.

"It might be refreshing."

"Maybe. But I'd probably have a difficult time swimming." She held up her sprained wrist.

"You're right." He turned her around in his arms until she was looking up into his familiar blue eyes. "How about a shower?"

"I have a better idea." She ran her good hand down his arm, entwining her fingers with his. "How about the bed?"

Holding his hand, she led him inside and down the hall to their bedroom. A bottle of champagne stood in an ice bucket beside the bed. "I guess you didn't have your heart set on a swim."

He gave her hand a gentle tug, drawing her into his arms. "I knew we'd end up here eventually."

"Hoping I'd drop my towel and climb onto your bed?"

"Yes." He claimed her mouth, kissing her deeply. "But I can't promise I'll keep my hands to myself this time."

"You'd better not," she said, glancing down at the splint on her arm. "With the way my arm feels, I don't think I can undress myself."

Eric stepped back, looking her over as if assessing her limitations. "That could be a problem."

"Eric, I'm fine," she said. "I'll just need a little help with my shirt and the button on my jeans."

He shook his head. "I don't know. The things I want to do to you…"

Her breath caught and she reached for the button on her jeans with her nondominant left hand. She struggled to release the top of her jeans, refusing to give up. Finally, she succeeded, pushing her pants down her legs.

"I'd hate to hurt you," he said. But he began unbuttoning his white dress shirt.

"You won't." Georgia managed to remove her underwear and toss them on the pile of clothes with her jeans. "I'm strong, remember?"

"I did promise I'd always believe in your inner strength, didn't I?" Eric pulled his undershirt over his head.

Georgia nodded, staring at his muscular chest as she struggled to pull her injured arm into her T-shirt. By the time she dropped her shirt on the floor, he'd discarded his pants and boxers. She swallowed, looking him over from head to toe.

It was as if they were back at the beginning. She ached to touch and explore the man she had loved for so long. More than anything, she wanted to make love to him. Just as she had that first night when she'd boldly walked into his room.

Only now she'd fallen in love with him. This wasn't about a moment in time, but the rest of her life. And her future looked as if he was one second away from tossing her on the bed and proving that he was anything but straightlaced.

Georgia reached her good hand behind her back and struggled with her bra. But she couldn't do it. "You don't really need to see my breasts, do you?"

"Yes, Georgia, I do." He closed the space between them until the fabric of her bra brushed against his chest.

With his two good hands, he released the hooks. He drew the shoulder straps down her arms, carefully navigating around her wrist. Then he stepped away, taking her bra with him.

"You're beautiful, Georgia." He tossed her bra aside. With one hand, he touched her chin, lifting her gaze to meet his. What she saw there—it wasn't playful and light-hearted. It was as if he was offering her a glance inside, at his heart and soul.

"Your outer beauty drew me in years ago," he said. "But it's your courage, your bravery, your resolve that won my heart. You asked me the other day if I was in love with you. And I was too much of a coward to acknowledge my feelings. I hid behind fear."

She lifted her good hand to his face, cupping his cheek. "You did what you thought was best for a little boy."

"No, I was afraid. And once I realized it…" He shook his head. "I didn't think I deserved you. But I want to try because you're what is best. For Nate and for me."

"I'm glad to hear that." She moved closer, pressing her naked body against his.

His arms wrapped around her, holding her close, his mouth brushing her ear. "Yes, Georgia. I'm in love with you. And I'm going to make sure you never doubt my love again."

She kissed his neck, his chest, anything she could reach, needing to feel his skin against her lips, while their limbs pressed tight. Eric. He was her rock, her stability, and her future. He was her friend. And now her lover. Always.

"Make love to me," she whispered, running her mouth up to his ear. "Please."

HOURS LATER, GEORGIA woke to the sound of the doorknob turning.

"Uncle Eric?" a small, tired voice called.

"Be right there, buddy." Eric gently lifted her head and slipped a pillow where his shoulder had been. "I'll be back."

"I'll be here," she promised. She watched as he pulled on his boxers and headed for the door.

Rolling onto her back, she stared at the ceiling, smiling. This was the beginning of the rest of her life. And right now she'd never felt so worthy of living, of returning home. That feeling might vanish tomorrow only to resurface again next week. She knew that. But for right now, she savored it. And if she continued to wonder why she'd lived, she'd have Eric by her side, loving her, supporting her—and that made the future look like a rainbow.

An hour later, maybe more, Eric returned and climbed into bed.

"Nate's asleep," he whispered.

"Good."

She let him wrap his arms around her. Resting her head on his chest, she closed her eyes. And finally, she fell asleep.

Epilogue

LIAM WALKED INTO the Moore Timber office in sneakers and clean clothes. It was the first time in months, maybe years, since he'd showed up without traces of the forest he'd been harvesting. But Georgia had given him an ultimatum: sit down with Eric and fix things, or else. He didn't want to face her "or else." He'd discovered over the past few weeks that his baby sister was a tiger—wild, sometimes skittish, and ridiculously fierce.

He found the door to Eric's office open. "Is now a good time?"

Eric looked up, his eyebrows raised in surprise. He hid it quickly behind a smile. Liam shook his head. Leave it to Georgia to keep this forced visit from her boyfriend.

"Sure. Come in." Eric stood and moved to the chairs in front of his desk. "Are you here for the results of the DOF investigation?"

Between learning his best friend had been sleeping with his sister (his hands formed fists again at the thought) and Georgia's accident, Liam had pushed the investigation to the back of his mind. He knew he was innocent. He didn't need the DOF or any other government organization to tell him that.

"No," he said. "But I would like to know where that son of a bitch started."

Eric gestured for him to sit, and he did, claiming the chair opposite his friend. "That's the good news," Eric said. "You were right. NOAA worked with the DOF to trace the fire back to a lightning strike on the other side of the hill. The wind blew sparks over to where you were harvesting, and from there, well, you know how the fire jumped all over the place."

"Good." Liam ran his hands through his hair, more relieved than he wanted to let on. "It still sucks that you needed a government organization to step in before you'd believe I followed the rules."

Eric leaned forward in his chair, resting his forearms on his thighs, his hands clasped tight between his knees. He kept his eyes downcast for a while, before looking up at Liam.

"I've made a lot of wrong choices lately," Eric admitted.

"Are you saying hooking up with my sister was a mistake? If you are, I swear I'm going to kick the shit out of you. Again."

"No. Letting her go was my mistake," he said. "And allowing you to walk away from Moore Timber. You can hate me all you want, but that doesn't change the fact that you're an asset to this company. Without you, I couldn't have built it up this far."

Liam sighed. "I don't hate you. Even if I wanted to, Georgia would kick my ass for holding a grudge. I got to admit that I hate the idea of her hooking up with anyone. But I guess you're better than most."

"Thanks, man." Eric smiled. "Makes what I'm about to say easier."

Liam's eyes narrowed. "If she's pregnant, I'll fucking—"

"No. Not where I was going with that." Eric raised his hands, palms out and open. "I wanted to talk to you about the business. I'm hoping you'll agree to take a bigger role. I need more time for Georgia and Nate. I don't want to work crazy hours, trying to keep all the bases covered. You've always done an excellent job running the crews. Now I'm asking you to move inside and help me run the company."

Liam frowned. "You want to park me behind a desk?"

"No. I want to offer you a piece of Moore Timber in exchange for taking a larger role. Some office work, yes. But you'll still be out there running chainsaws."

"Equity?" Liam blinked, trying to hide his surprise. Moore Timber had always been Eric's baby, not his. Sure, Liam worked his ass off day after day, but Eric knew the business side. Liam didn't. "You're sure about this?"

"Yeah. You deserve it."

"You swear Georgia's not pregnant?" he said, because shit, this sounded like the kind of offer a man made before he told his friend he'd knocked up his sister.

Eric smiled. "Not yet. One step at a time. First, I'm going to marry her."

"I hope you'll do that with or without the promise of more kids," Liam said. "I'm still trying to erase the mental picture of you two in your kitchen from my mind—"

"I'm sorry," Eric said, his tone leaving no doubt he was 100 percent sincere. "You never should have seen that."

"But," Liam continued, "you helped her move on. I couldn't do that. I wanted to, but I couldn't see past her wild thrill rides. I've been walking around terrified she'd decide to go back. To the army." He shook his head. "But now she has you."

"She's not leaving," Eric said firmly.

"Yeah, and I think your ways of keeping her here are better than my plans to lock her in my spare bedroom. Not that I want details."

Eric smiled, leaning back in his chair. "So we're good? You'll accept the offer?"

"You mean will I take part of your company?" Liam clapped his hands together. "Hell, yes."

"Part of the company for a bigger role in the business," Eric reminded him. "I'm handing you a lot of extra hours."

"I think I can handle it."

"Good." Eric stood and picked up a file from his desk. "I'm looking to buy Summers Family Trucking. They're struggling financially right now." He held out the folder. "Here are their numbers."

Liam took the folder. "We'd benefit from having our own operation instead of relying on contractors. No question about it."

"Especially after what happened with B&B."

Liam nodded, pretending to read through the numbers on the pages. He didn't understand half of it, partly because his mind could focus on only one thing. "Summers Family Trucking, huh?"

Eric leaned against the front of his desk, his arms crossed in front of him. "Will that be a problem?"

"Might be for them."

"I'm guessing they're going to overlook the past," Eric said. "They'll go under if they don't sell, and we're their only option."

Liam nodded. "And they're probably jumping at the chance to sell to you. They can trust you won't send everyone packing and sell the company for parts. But they probably won't like that fact that I'm part of the equation now."

"You've been my number two for years. They know that. And the way you left things with Katie—you didn't do anything wrong back then."

"Brothers are funny when it comes to their sisters."

"I know." Eric ran a hand over the faded bruises on his face. "In any other situation, I'd never let you land those punches."

"You hurt Georgia in any way, and we'll find out."

Eric sobered. "I love her and I'm going to take care of her. Always."

"I know you will."

All those years ago, he'd tried to do the same by Katie. But it had blown up in his face. He wanted a second chance. And it wasn't the threat of a three-against-one fight with her brothers that was keeping him from trying. When he went after her, he wanted to be sure she'd say yes.

"When I said I planned to marry Georgia first?" Eric said, drawing Liam's thoughts away from the past. "I'm going to ask her. Soon. I'd like your blessing."

Liam stared long and hard at the man he'd considered his best friend since he was a kid, the man his little sister had turned to after all the shit she'd been through in the army.

"You have it."

GEORGIA DANCED THROUGH the kitchen, a mixing bowl in one hand and a wooden spoon in the other. On the radio, a pop star she'd read about in magazines sang about a woman getting knocked down by life and pushing herself up, fighting and staying strong. She kept the music low so that she didn't wake Nate as she twirled, pausing when she heard the sound of the garage door.

Eric. He was home.

She kept stirring, determined to finish the brownies so that Nate could take them to school in the morning. The door opened as she poured the batter into a glass dish.

"You're baking again," Eric said.

"Brownies. But this time I used a mix from a box."

Out of the corner of her eye, she watched him set his briefcase down and walk over to her. "Not worried about competing with the other moms?"

"Nope," she said. "But I did add beet juice so that I can pretend they're a little healthy."

Eric laughed, looping his arm around her. "Nice. But I have to admit, I like it better when you're wearing the chocolate."

"I might have picked up some Hershey's syrup at the store," she admitted.

"Georgia."

She loved it when he growled her name. And right now, he was so close she felt the word against her ear. Smiling, she broke free from his hold to place the brownies in the preheated oven. "First, I need to finish these."

"How long will they bake?"

"Not long enough for what you're thinking." She closed the oven and turned to face him. "How was your day?"

Shaking his head, Eric drew her close. Pressed up against him, she could tell he liked the idea of chocolate syrup in bed. She glanced at the oven clock. Only twenty-two more minutes…

"Liam came to see me," he said. "But I suspect you knew that, seeing as you sent him."

"Hmm, I might have. You told him about the investigation, right?" She looped her arms around his neck. "And gave him his job back?"

He smiled down at her. "I gave him part of the company."

Her eyes widened. "You didn't have to do that."

"Yeah, I did. I want to spend more time at home. Here. With you."

Georgia stiffened. It felt as if a storm cloud had descended and was now hovering over her head, threatening and ominous. She'd been feeling so sure, so steady since she'd moved back into Eric's home. "Eric, I'm fine. I thought…I thought you trusted me not to bolt in the middle of the night."

"I do." His hands moved to her face, cupping her cheeks as his blue eyes stared down at her. "Believe me, I do. That's not the reason."

"If it's about the nightmares—"

"Georgia, shh." Eric pressed a finger to her lips. "I don't think you're going to leave, and I'm confident we can handle it if your scary bears come back."

Looking up at him, she saw excitement and nervous energy brewing. The storm clouds dissipated, replaced by desire.

"I wanted to wait until we were at the coast," he said, never once looking away, "and do this right."

"Do what right?"

His hands fell away from her face as he lowered to one knee, right there in the middle of the kitchen. "Georgia," he said, taking her hand and looking up at her, "will you marry me? Will you let me love you forever? And promise to love me back?"

Georgia sank to her knees beside him on the floor, her hands locked in his. She studied the familiar face of the friend, now lover, who'd always been there for her, who'd opened her eyes to trust and love, who saw her strengths, and held her hand when she needed someone to lean on. Inside, feelings swelled and she clung to the emotions, no longer afraid to love Eric. Forever.

"Yes."

Coming in September 2014

Caught in the Act

Book Two: Independence Falls

Falling for his rivals' little sister could cost him everything…

Liam Trulane is determined to strike a deal with Summers Family Trucking to buy the business and make it a part of Moore Timber. Only problem? After Liam's relationship with their little sister, Katie, went south years ago, the Summers brothers are more enemy than friend. If both parties can set the past aside, they can close the deal. But when Katie welcomes him back into her life and her bed, Liam risks everything to make Katie his.

After Liam betrayed her trust, Katie Summers will do anything to keep him from walking away with the family business. She decides to seduce Liam, knowing that when her brothers find out, they will back off from the deal. And she'll finally have her revenge. But when her plan spirals out of control, Katie learns that payback might come at too high a price, demanding both her heart and her independence.

About the Author

After several years on the other side of the publishing industry, **SARA JANE STONE** bid good-bye to her sales career to pursue her dream—writing romance novels. Sara Jane resides in Brooklyn, New York, with her very supportive real-life hero, two lively young children, and a lazy Burmese cat. Visit her online at www.sarajanestone.com, or find her on Facebook at Sara Jane Stone.

Join Sara Jane's newsletter to receive new-release information, news about contests, giveaways, and more! To subscribe, visit www.sarajanestone.com and look for her newsletter entry form.

Visit www.AuthorTracker.com for exclusive information on your favorite HarperCollins authors.

Give in to your impulses . . .
Read on for a sneak peek at five brand-new
e-book original tales of romance
from Avon Books.
Available now wherever e-books are sold.

WHITE COLLARED
PART ONE: MERCY
By Shelly Bell

WINNING MISS WAKEFIELD
THE WALLFLOWER WEDDING SERIES
By Vivienne Lorret

INTOXICATED
A BILLIONAIRE BACHELORS CLUB NOVELLA
By Monica Murphy

ONCE UPON A HIGHLAND AUTUMN
By Lecia Cornwall

THE GUNSLINGER
By Lorraine Heath

An Excerpt from

WHITE COLLARED
PART ONE: MERCY

by Shelly Bell

In Shelly Bell's four-part serialized erotic thriller, a young law student enters a world of dark secrets and seductive fantasies when she goes undercover at an exclusive sex club in order to prove her client is not guilty of murder.

After three hours of computer research on piercing the corporate veil, Kate's vision blurred, the words on the screen bleeding into one another until they resembled a giant Rorschach inkblot. She lowered her mug of lukewarm coffee to her cubicle's mahogany tabletop and rubbed her tired eyes.

Without warning, the door to the interns' windowless office flew open, banging against the wall. Light streamed into the dim room, casting the elongated shadow of her boss, Nicholas Trenton, on the beige carpet.

"Ms. Martin, take your jacket and come with me." He didn't wait for a response, simply issued his command and strode down the hall.

Jumping to her feet, she teetered on her secondhand heels and grabbed her suit jacket from the back of her chair. As Mr. Trenton's intern for the year, she'd follow him off the edge of a cliff. She had no choice in the matter if she wanted a junior associate position at Detroit's most prestigious law firm, Joseph and Long, after graduation. Because of the fierce competition for an internship and because several qualified lackeys waited patiently in the wings for an opening, one minor screwup would result in termination.

Most of the other interns ignored the interruption, but

her best friend Hannah took a second to raise an arched eyebrow. Kate shrugged, having no idea what her boss required. He hadn't spoken to her since her initial interview a few months earlier.

She collected her briefcase, her heart pounding. As far as she knew, she hadn't made a mistake since starting two months ago. Other than class time, she'd spent virtually every waking moment at this firm, a schedule her boyfriend, Tom, resented.

She raced as fast as she could down the hallway and found her boss pacing and talking on his cell phone in the marbled lobby. He frowned and pointedly looked at his watch, demonstrating his displeasure at her delay. Still on the phone, he stalked out of the firm and headed toward the elevator. She chased him, cursing her short legs as she remained a step or two behind until catching up with him on the elevator.

When the doors slid shut, he ended his call and slipped his cell into the pocket of his Armani jacket. She risked a quick glance at him to ascertain his mood, careful not to visually suggest anything more than casual regard.

He was an extremely handsome man whose picture frequently appeared in local magazines and papers beside prominent judges and legislative officials. But photos couldn't do him justice, film lacking the capability of capturing his commanding presence. Often she'd had to fight her instinct to look directly into his blue eyes. At the office, his every move, his every word overshadowed anyone and everything around her.

Standing close to him in the claustrophobic space, she inhaled the musky scent of his aftershave, felt his radiating heat.

Mr. Trenton spoke, fracturing the quiet of the small space with his deep and powerful voice. "This morning, our firm's biggest client, Jaxon Deveroux, arrived home from his business trip and found his wife dead from multiple stab wounds."

Once the elevator doors opened, they stepped out into the bustling main floor lobby, and she fought to match Mr. Trenton's brisk pace as they headed toward the parking garage. "While typically I would refer my clients to Jeffrey Reaver, the head of our criminal division, Mr. Deveroux and I have been friends for many years, and he requested me personally. Jaxon's a very private man, but those who are in his circle are aware of certain . . . proclivities that may come up in the police's line of questioning."

What sort of proclivities?

An Excerpt from

WINNING MISS WAKEFIELD
The Wallflower Wedding Series
by Vivienne Lorret

When her betrothed suddenly announces his plans
to marry another, Merribeth Wakefield knows
only a bold move will bring him back and restore
her tattered reputation: She must take a lesson
in seduction from a master of the art. But when
the dark and brooding rake, Lord Knightswold,
takes her under his wing, her education quickly
goes from theory to hands-on practice, and her
heart is given a crash course in true desire!

"Now, give back my handkerchief," Lord Knightswold said, holding out his hand as he returned to her side. "You're the sort to keep it as a memento. I cannot bear the thought of my handkerchief being worshipped by a forlorn Miss by moonlight or tucked away with mawkish reverence beneath a pillow."

The portrait he painted was so laughable that she smiled, heedless of exposing her flaw. "You flatter yourself. Here." She dropped it into his hand as she swept past him, prepared to leave. "I have no desire to touch it a moment longer. I will leave you to your pretense of sociability."

" 'Tis no pretense. I have kept good company this evening." Either the brandy had gone to her head, impairing her hearing, or he actually sounded sincere.

She paused and rested her hands on the carved rosewood filigree edging the top of the sofa. "Much to my own folly. I never should have listened to Lady Eve Sterling. It was her lark that sent me here."

He feigned surprise. "Oh? How so?"

If it weren't for the brandy, she would have left by now. Merribeth rarely had patience for such games, and she knew his question was part of a game he must have concocted with

Eve. However, his company had turned out to be exactly the diversion she'd needed, and she was willing to linger. "She claimed to have forgotten her reticule and sent me here to fetch it—no doubt wanting me to find you."

He looked at her as if confused.

"I've no mind to explain it to you. After all, you were abetting her plot, lying in wait, here on this very sofa." She brushed her fingers over the smooth fabric, thinking of him lying there in the dark. "Not that I blame you. Lady Eve is difficult to say no to. However, I will conceal the truth from her, and we can carry on as if her plan had come to fruition. It would hardly have served its purpose anyway."

He moved toward her, his broad shoulders outlined by the distant torchlight filtering in through the window behind him. "Refresh my memory then. What was it I was supposed to do whilst in her employ?"

She blushed again. Was he going to make her say the words aloud? No gentleman would.

So of course *he* would. She decided to get it over with as quickly as possible. "She professed that a kiss from a rake could instill confidence and mend a broken heart."

He stopped, impeded by the sofa between them. His brow lifted in curiosity. "Have you a broken heart in need of mending?"

The deep murmur of his voice, the heated intensity in his gaze—and quite possibly the brandy—all worked against her better sense and sent those tingles dancing in a pagan circle again.

Oh, yes, the thought as she looked up at him. *Yes, Lord Knightswold. Mend my broken heart.*

However, her mouth intervened. "I don't believe so." She gasped at the realization. "I should, you know. After five years, my heart should be in shreds. Shouldn't it?"

He turned before she could read his expression and then sat down on the sofa, affording her a view of the top of his head. "I know nothing of broken hearts, or their mending."

"Pity," she said, distracted by the dark silken locks that unexpectedly brushed her fingers. "Neither do I."

However accidental the touch of his hair had been, now her fingers threaded through the fine strands with untamed curiosity and blatant disregard for propriety.

Lord Knightswold let his head fall back, permitting—perhaps even encouraging—her to continue. She did, without thought to right, wrong, who he was, or who she was supposed to be. Running both hands through his hair, massaging his scalp, she watched his eyes drift closed.

Then, Merribeth Wakefield did something she never intended to do.

She kissed a rake.

An Excerpt from

INTOXICATED
A Billionaire Bachelors Club Novella
by Monica Murphy

It's Gage and Marina's wedding day, but wedded
bliss seems a long way off: Ivy's just gone into labor,
Marina's missing her matron of honor, and Bryn's
giving Matt the silent treatment. It's up to Archer,
Gage, and Matt to make sure this day goes off
without a hitch. But between brides and babies,
there's the not-so-little issue of the million-dollar
bet to attend to. If only they can figure out who
won . . . and who's paying up. Is everyone a winner?
Or will someone leave broke—and brokenhearted?

Gage

I'm a freaking mess.

"Calm down, dude," Matt whispers out of the side of his mouth. We're standing so close our shoulders are practically touching. Wonder whether he'd catch me if I fell. "You look like you're gonna drop."

"I *feel* like I'm gonna drop," I tell him, sounding like an idiot but not really caring. He's my new best man, so I need him to step it up. If I pass out, it's on him.

"Your girl is going to make her appearance at any minute." Matt nods toward the beginning of the aisle, where no one stands. Where are the girls? We already made our walk down the aisle, Matt taking Marina's mom to her seat, me leading my mother.

"Hope she shows up soon," I mutter, meaning it. I feel antsy. My suit is too tight. My throat is dry. I'm dying for a drink. Preferably booze.

Probably not a good idea.

The flower girl suddenly struts down the aisle, cute as can be in a white lacy gown. Louisa is one of Marina's cousins. She has about a bazillion of them.

Almost all of them are sitting in the crowd, watching me. Probably pissed because Marina and I both agreed that we didn't want a huge, ridiculous wedding party. We blew their chance to wear bridesmaids' gowns.

Then Bryn appears, a freaking vision in pale yellow. She walks down the aisle slowly, a coy smile on her face as she shoots me a glance, then trains her gaze on Matt. As her smile disappears, her eyes widen, and I look at Matt, who's staring at Bryn like she's the most beautiful creature he's ever seen in his life.

Poor dude is straight up in love with Bryn. Like, a complete and total goner. I get what he's feeling.

The music fades, and a new song starts, a low, melodic tune played to perfection by the small group of musicians set up off to the right. I straighten my spine, clasp my hands behind my back as I wait for my bride to make her appearance.

And then . . . there she is. Her arm curls around her father's, he looking respectably intimidating in his tuxedo. A frothy veil covers her face, and the skirt of her gown is wide, nearly as wide as the aisle they're walking down.

Tears threaten, and I blink once. Hard. Damn it, I'm not going to cry. I'm happy, not sad. But I'm also overwhelmed, filled with love for this woman who's about to become my partner in life.

They approach and stop just before us, turning to each other so her father can lift the veil, revealing her face to me for the first time. He leans in and kisses her cheek as the minister asks who gives this woman to this man, just as we rehearsed yesterday. Her father says, *I do*, his deep voice a little shaky and my sympathy goes out to him.

I'm still feeling pretty shaky myself.

Marina steps up to stand beside me and I take her hand, unable to stop from leaning in and brushing a quick kiss against her cheek. "You look beautiful," I murmur, my voice just as unsteady as her dad's.

But I don't care. I have no shame. I'm getting married, damn it. I'm allowed to cry. To smile. To laugh. I'm making this woman mine.

Forever.

An Excerpt from

ONCE UPON A HIGHLAND AUTUMN

by Lecia Cornwall

Legends say a curse lurks among the shattered
stones of Glen Dorian Castle. Will the love
that is beginning to grow between Megan and
Kit be able to withstand fate? For only the
living, those with bold hearts and true love,
can restore peace to Glen Dorian at last.

Megan scanned the valley once more and ignored her sister. "I'm just saying goodbye to Glenlorne. At least for now."

"Better to say farewell to people than places," Sorcha said. "I've already been to the village, telling folk I'll be back come spring." She grinned mischievously at her sister. "You won't, though—you'll be in London, bothered by the attentions of all those daft English lairds at your first Season."

Megan felt a rush of irritation. "Lords, Sorcha, not lairds—and stop teasing," she commanded, and flounced down the steep path that led back to the castle.

Sorcha picked a flower and skipped beside her sister like a mountain goat. One by one, she plucked at the petals. "How many English *lords* will Megan McNabb kiss?" she asked, dancing around her sister. "One . . . two . . . three . . ."

"Stop it," Megan said, and snatched the flower away. She wouldn't kiss anyone but Eachann. But her sister picked another flower.

"How many English lords will come and ask Alec for Meggy's delicate hand in marriage?" she mused, but Megan snatched that blossom too, before Sorcha could begin counting again.

"I shan't go to London, and I will never marry an English lord," she said fiercely.

"We'll see what mama says to that," Sorcha replied. "And Muira would say never is a very long time indeed."

Megan stopped. "What exactly did Muira say?" she asked. Old Muira had the sight, or so it was said.

Sorcha grinned like a pirate and rubbed a dusty hand over her face, leaving a dark smudge. "I thought you didn't believe in the old ways."

Megan rolled her eyes, let her gaze travel up the smooth green slopes of the hills to their rocky crests, and thought of the legends and tales, the old stories, the belief that magic made its home in the glen.

Of course she believed.

She believed so much that she'd decided to become the keeper of the old tales when Glenlorne's ancient *seannachaidh* had died the previous winter without leaving a successor. She loved to hear the old stories, and she planned to write them down so they'd never be lost. But for now, in Sorcha's annoying company, she raised her chin. Now was hardly the time to be fanciful. "Of course I don't believe in magic. I think being sensible is far more likely to get you what you want—not counting flower petals or relying on the seeings of an old woman."

"Muira foresaw an Englishman, and a treasure," Sorcha said, not deterred one whit by talk of sense. "Right there in the smoke of the fire, clear as day."

Megan felt her mouth dry. "For me?" she asked through stiff lips.

"She didn't know that. For one of us, surely."

Megan let out a sigh of relief. Perhaps she was safe. If only Muira had seen Eachann, riding home, his heart light, his purse heavy, with a fine gold ring in his pocket. "That's the trouble with Muira's premonitions. She sees things but can't say what they mean."

"Still, a treasure would be nice," Sorcha chirped. "A chest of gold, or a cache of pearls and rubies—"

"Not if it comes with an Englishman attached," Megan muttered.

An Excerpt from

THE GUNSLINGER

by *Lorraine Heath*

(A version of this work originally appeared in
the print anthology *To Tame a Texan*, under
the title "Long Stretch of Lonesome")

Chance Wilder never wanted to be a hero. That
is, until a young boy offers Chance everything he
owns to rescue his sister from a couple of thugs.
But after he saves her, Lillian Madison awakens
in him long-buried dreams and possibilities.
Facing the demons of his past, Chance is forced to
question his next move. Dare he risk everything
by following his heart . . . and trust that the
road to redemption begins with Lillian?

"Why do you want me in the house?"

"As payment," she blurted, the heat flaming her face. "Payment for your kindness to Toby . . . and for saving me. I hate that you killed the man—" Tears burned the backs of her eyes. She despised the weakness that made her sink to the porch. She wrapped her arms around herself and rocked back and forth, memories of the glittering lust and hatred burning in Wade's eyes assailing her. "He was going . . . going to . . . no one would have stopped him."

Strong arms embraced her, and she pressed her head against the warm, sturdy chest. She heard the constant thudding of his heart.

"No one wants you here. Why don't you leave?" he asked in a low rumble.

She shook her head. "This place was the only gift Jack Ward ever gave me. It's special to me."

"You loved him?" he asked quietly.

She nodded her head jerkily. "I shouldn't have. God knows I should have despised him, but I could never bring myself to hate him. Even now, when his gift brings me such pain, I can't overlook the fact that he gave it to me out of love."

"Have you ever talked with John Ward, tried to settle the differences?"

"No. John came here one night with an army of men. He told me to pack up and get, then threatened to kill me as a trespasser if I ever set foot on his land. Delivered his message and rode out. Makes it hard to reason with a man when you can't get near him."

"It's even harder to reason with him if he's dead."

Lillian's heart slammed against her ribs. Trembling, she clutched Wilder's shirt and lifted her gaze to his, trying to see into the depths of his silver eyes. But his eyes were only shadows hidden by the night. His embrace was steady, secure, his hands slowly trailing up and down her back. "Promise me you won't kill him," she demanded.

A silence stretched between them, as though he was weighing the promise against the offer that he'd cloaked as a simple statement. "If he's dead, you and the boy will be safe."

She tightened her fingers around his shirt and gave him a small shake. "I don't want the blood of Jack Ward's son on my hands. Give me your word that you won't kill him."

His hands stilled. "What are you willing to pay me to keep me from killing him?"

Her stomach knotted, and her chest ached with a tightness that threatened to suffocate her. Even though she couldn't see it clearly, she felt the intensity of his perusal. She had no money, nothing to offer him—nothing to offer a killer except herself. And she knew he was aware of that fact.

Had she actually begun to feel sympathy for this man whose solitary life gave him no roots, allowed him no love? He was worse than Wade because at least Wade had barreled into her, announcing loudly and clearly what he wanted of her. The killer wanted the same thing, but he'd lured her into caring for him and trusting him, catching her heart unawares.

The pain of betrayal ripped through her, and she thought she might actually understand why one man would kill another. Tiny shudders coursed through her body, and tears stung her eyes as she answered hoarsely, "Anything."

Beneath her clutched hand, his heart increased its tempo, pounding harder and faster. He cradled her face between his powerful hands. "Anything?" he whispered. "Even if I want all a woman can offer?"

She nodded jerkily. "I don't want John Ward killed." How could she warn the man when approaching him meant her certain death?

Wilder leaned closer to her. His warm breath fanned her face. He shifted his thumbs and gently stroked the corners of her mouth. "Give you my word that I'll let the bastard live."

He pressed his mouth to hers, demanding, claiming all that she'd offered to willingly pay: her body, her heart, her soul. She could not give one without giving the others.